I0591419

Capturing the Butterfly

Sharon K. Grosh

Black Rose Writing | Texas

First printing

This is a work of fiction. Names, characters, businesses, places, events, and incidents are either the products of the author's imagination or used in a fictitious manner. Any resemblance to actual persons, living or dead, or actual events is purely coincidental.

ISBN: 978-1-68433-852-8
PUBLISHED BY BLACK ROSE WRITING
www.blackrosewriting.com

Printed in the United States of America
Suggested Retail Price (SRP) $17.95

Capturing the Butterfly is printed in EB Garamond

*As a planet-friendly publisher, Black Rose Writing does its best to eliminate unnecessary waste to reduce paper usage and energy costs, while never compromising the reading experience. As a result, the final word count vs. page count may not meet common expectations.

Cover design by Hannah Cunningham
http://www.behance.net/OddJobArt_Cunningham

With much gratitude and love,
I dedicate this book to:

My Parents, Toni and Wes
Both avid readers.

"*Capturing the Butterfly* takes the reader on an adventure through the past and future, as we consider the importance of following our hearts and the power of unexpected friendships."
–Nora Murray, author of *Kingdom Come*

"A surrealistic romp through time and imagination, distilled through the words and wisdom of a delightful pink bear!"
–JR Konkol, author of *Gathering the Fallen*

"A wildly imaginative, shape-shifting, time-traveling, multi-cultural (and multi-species) re-generation of history."
–Geneen Haugen, with writings appearing in many journals and books, including *Spiritual Ecology: The Cry of the Earth; Thomas Berry: Dreamer of the Earth; Parabola; Ecopsychology Journal; DailyGood.org; Kosmos Journal; and High Country News*

"Sharon K. Grosh's *Capturing the Butterfly* brings three disparate characters to a remote world filled with mystery and beauty. Although each is focused on a quest, their stories intertwine, blurring the lines between how their actions drive their own quest, and how they affect others."
–Mary Ann Noe, author of *To Know Her*

Capturing
the Butterfly

CHAPTER 1

Telling my story is not easy, but it must be told. It is both big and small, affecting world history and changing my life forever. If you knew the story as well as I do, you would agree. This story started in a snowstorm. I am serious about story-telling and will reveal the story carefully in order for you to suspend judgement as long as possible.

Record-breaking winters always have one snowstorm that is beyond comprehension, especially if you are living inside of it. Heavy white flakes silently drop from some place that never stops pushing them out. The quiet falling of these white crystals load the tops of trees, bending them over in a death spiral. Winter is a savage event.

I was conscious of the cold and snow shielding me from intrusion. While I was safe, the presence of many bears that stayed before me also gave my mind comfort. This was a perfect, time-tested location for deep sleep.

Curled far away from the entrance, my body was safe. Unless I sensed danger, I reacted slowly to most disturbances. What a contrast from summer when I moved forward, never retreating, always aware of the earth that I stepped on. But safety always was the backbone of hibernation and I was not worried. While my body welcomed the rest, my mind wandered. I was not awake, but sometimes roamed the woods in my sleep. Dream sleep could trick me into thinking I was awake.

Body fat erodes slowly, systematically disappearing, leaving a lighter, thinner cloak of protection from cold. The walls of the cave surrounded me, another insulated layer, as my fat-bank slowly disappeared. The crisp, dense air of the cave was part of the special alchemy that kept me, and all of my ancestors before me, alive. In my corner, I was content to protect my reserves until there was nothing left. Spring-life then takes over. Other than the occasional small animal that passed through this cave, nothing would dare penetrate my layers in this protected space.

My heart was slow, to the beat of snow falling in my winter dreams. I felt heavy, relaxed and peaceful; a state of serenity that sustained me. I was dreaming about rambling around outside, with the snow quietly swirling and building gentle white walls in strange patterns. I felt this impenetrable fortress around me as I parted the snow curtain in front of me.

That was the dream I remembered when I woke up to a raised heartbeat. An awakened heart accelerates at a pace that depletes stored resources and signifies danger. What was the danger?

There was a sound. It was the soft crunch of frozen snow, possibly a small animal seeking shelter. The pace was slow, but not stealth-like. It was more intentional, placing each step carefully. I heard a few more steps, followed by a long pause. The pause meant the animal was feeling fear. Good. This animal must detect my presence. Smells are deterrents to the wise. I relaxed back into sleep-without-dreaming.

Branches breaking across the entrance woke me again. They were arranged carefully to alert me of intrusion. These branches determined the weight and agility of the intruder, even through drifting snow. This time, the intruder had a unique sound. The branches were cracking as if the intruder slid deep into it, without the skill to rebound. Human? My heart raced faster. All senses were on high alert as the creature struggled to escape the thorns lying in the deepest layer of the opening to the cave.

There are few four-legged animals on earth that would get stuck in a branch pile and continue to struggle, making things worse. Four legs are powerful in escaping where humans are limited. As my mind thought about the possibilities of what kind of animal was disturbing my sleep, I was sure I was safe. This animal was small and stupid. A bad combination against a bear of my size.

I fell back asleep until another noise woke me up a third time. My heartbeat was not elevated so I opened only one eye. I saw a vague shadow, sitting still, at the mouth of the cave. My heart sprinted to full capacity. It was human, with long, smooth black hair concealing a robe the color of the rare bluebird. I opened my second eye and could see the complete figure of a small human, maybe female. She sat with her back to the cave. I did not smell fear, but I could hear each beat her heart made. It was faster than mine, but I was catching up to her. Why wasn't she moving? Does she know I'm here? She must smell my musk I smell her; she smells like blossoms, maybe apple. The smell made me sleepy.

Did I fall asleep? I woke again and she was now facing into the cave. I slammed my right paw forward against the dry ground. She jumped up, squinting to see into the cave, then looking behind her as if being chased. I knew the exact moment when she saw me. This extraordinary creature was facing me directly, as her eyes carefully panned my body. She stopped, locked on my two eyes that beamed back to her. Was she frightened? Was the outside danger greater than this cave? She closed both eyes and opened them, looking at me. A slight movement away from the snow barrier gave her a purposeful look. Why wasn't she frightened? How long has it been since I dreamed? I must be dreaming again.

The strong smell of the apple blossoms, heavy with humidity, filled the cave. This lingering smell was pleasant. She stood motionless, tree branches sticking out of her head. Her white socks had a lizard-like gap at the big toe. The space was packed with ice balls between her toes. She held shoes, made from wood, in her hands, hands that were as red as her face. Her smile was soft, and I now realized that she was small for a human, the size of a very young bear. A heavy sigh came out of her mouth as her lips turned up and exuded a fresh ginger smell that enveloped the whole cave. I started to move my body slowly to a sitting position and her eyes continued to fix on mine as she followed my movements carefully. I raised my paw upward, in acceptance, as she sat down.

As I think of this first meeting, and all that happened since, I am struck with my acceptance of her without having a physical response to danger. In extreme situations, it was possible to come out of hibernation quickly, as each muscle fiber in a bear body can seethe with an instant supply of oxygen. That important element would transfer to my legs, moving them urgently and aggressively. I could be angry and violent, lashing my claws at anything violating my space. This was different.

Once, a fox entered our cave during the deep winter sleep and Mother woke up first. She opened her large mouth and uttered a sound that would melt snow. Fox were unusually agile and fast, but this fox froze, unable to move with Mother's ability to immobilize creatures with her eyes. It was her special talent. She held that fox in her mouth and I could hear a bone break, causing the fox to loosen and fall limp against her mighty jaw. Lily, my twin sister, was frightened, but I stood up and watched. Mother left the cave with the body in her jaw and returned to coax us back to sleep.

I sat and watched as this small human took off her socks and laid them next to her wicker basket. While I was still a little foggy in the head from the strong scent that encompassed the cave, I was calmly watching her. She stood up, only half as high as the cave, and gathered wood from piles I left around. She assembled each piece of wood, leaning one against another, all pointing to the ceiling. With amazing speed, she reached into her robe, brought out wooden matchsticks and scraped the stone wall with such vigor, I fell back on my haunches. The fire burned quickly from the crisp, dry wood. The ancient cave moved the swirling smoke up the air shaft and there was a bronze light, spreading heat through the dense frigid air. There were a million sparks moving around the cave. She started to drip water from her elbows, forming a pool around her body.

Her dark, black eyes and long lashes against a pale, white face did not remind me of a human. Sitting still inside her cloak of blue, she reminded me of a deep pool of water. The ground had a natural bowl shape I used for capturing water during the spring melt. It served her purpose as she folded herself into the small space. Finally, she stopped looking at me and focused on the fire. Her shoulders relaxed slightly, as her neck grew longer, fitting with her straight up and down posture.

Why was she here? In my cave? As in a dream, the question sounded foreign, passing through me with little impact. This dream was different, uncomfortable, but not threatening. I was acting like this was natural, like being with my sister or my mother. Having developed a lifelong fear of humans, why was I accepting such a creature?

The fire reflected off my large body and rapidly warmed the room. But this was not a perfect moment and I needed to pay attention. The girl was not afraid, upset, nervous or troubled. She was not demanding, attacking and definitely not banging around. Her smell of ginger and blossoms still lingered.

As I tried to shake my head to awaken from the dream, she stood up. She pulled out a fan from her robe and opened it with an efficient snap. She meant business. I watched her place her basket in front of her. From it, she removed a pot and carried it to the cave entrance. Expertly, she scooped snow into the vessel and arranged it on the coals with gentle grace. She carefully removed two bowls from the basket. Reaching into her pockets again, she pulled dried leaves from a pouch, which added to the intoxicating atmosphere that enveloped the cave. She laid black fabric on the flattest surface of the dirt floor and fit the small bowl on top of the large one. Each movement was smooth, gliding seamlessly with undeniable confidence in what she was doing. Finally, adding the crisp leaves to the hot water, she placed a cover on the pot and expertly scooped up more charcoal from around the fire, placing it around the pot. Always moving in a flow, she established a smaller area for arranging things from her many pockets. These smooth movements gave me the memory of swans swimming in my lake, with their necks bent at an angle that defined grace. This was a dream! While this dream was pleasant enough, I still had a problem with it.

I recall drinking my first tea. She handed me the large bowl and let go once I wrapped my paws around it. My instinct was to bend over and use my tongue. I tried to copy what she did, raising the bowl to my mouth. This movement was difficult and unnatural. It would be much easier to lick the water on the ground. But there was something very soothing as I watched her open her mouth around the rim of the bowl. As I look back at this moment, it was the first in many efforts at learning human ways. I worked on raising the bowl, bringing it to my mouth and not using my tongue. She nodded and words came from her mouth that were no more threatening than a bird song. The actions seemed to lower my heart rate and I relaxed. By the time I placed the bowl on the ground, in front of me, I was exhausted but no liquid remained. She stood up, moved very close to me to pick up the bowl and returned to the place she created. The dream I was living was unusual and I truly wanted to wake up. Not reacting to an intrusion like this was not natural.

After that, she put the bowls away in the wicker basket and the tea was placed in one of her many pockets. She added wood to the fire, causing a large flare, and the cave now felt like a warm summer day. This young creature was sitting up, still tightly bundled within her wrap of sapphire folds. She stretched and yawned and pulled a mat out to lie on within inches of the fire. She put her head down, closed her eyes and was asleep. I gradually fell to sleep too. I do not know for how long.

CHAPTER 2

Morning light held a magical atmosphere, created by drifts of snow enclosing the cave in stillness. The quiet was complemented by sunlight filtering through each crystal of ice caked across the entrance. The curtain of ligh sparkled as it bounced against the cave wall. When I see light play against the cave walls, I want to stay motionless just to watch. Hibernation brings these moments out of me. I'm inside and outside of my body as I focus on breathing. The air swirled ashes that rose from the fire, now cold, creating a scene almost too beautiful to describe.

I still remember that moment before things changed for me permanently. With my altered ability to translate thoughts into words, I can continue this story.

As I looked around at the sparkles bouncing off the walls, I noticed a small mound of blue and white engulfing my intruder. She was purring in her sleep. I remembered the rare bird that shows up in blue each spring. Mother taught us how to be still, to carefully observe details of everything, and to keep learning the ways of all creatures.

Her presence was troubling. Was I dreaming? There was a living human right here, in the cave, asleep.

She made a pleasant sound, enhanced by the delightful smell of blossoms. Her small feet stuck outside of the robe and were surrounded by teardrop puddles from the snow that melted. The sun light left crystal patterns on her face. I was watching this blue bird stretch and open her eyes. She was not threatening me. Danger can come in various disguises, but she became my blue bird that I could quietly sit and watch.

She started to move out of her nest, thrusting a hand out from the many fabrics surrounding her. She pressed her hand against the dirt with a spiral motion from her waist. She moved forward and backward while she stood up, no longer bracing her hands against the floor. I watched as she fanned her arm about in a strange, slow motion dance. I recognized the dance, as similar to what birds do in the spring. I studied her, while she repeated the movement several times, touching the ground with one hand and reaching upward with another. Then as she twisted her body, both hands came together and rested on her stomach. It was a simple movement and I loved watching her switch sides each time. Maybe she was not a human at all, but the large bird we call crane. I decided to just enjoy this dream and not fight it.

Our experience with humans involved studying them in order to avoid them. Mother gave lots of advice on the habits of humans to me and my sister. If we heard a loud shot, we would automatically move in a direction away from the sound. Mother showed more concern for me than my sister. I knew she was concerned that the color of my fur made me stand out, like the blue bird. I was a color rarely seen in the woods, more rare than blue. There was no place for me to go except away from humans. Once they saw me, they would find me and kill me. Mother was clear about that. All bears had coats of fur that blended with most trees, especially oak trees. I did not have the advantage of concealment. But Mother found many ways to protect me from humans, hiding me, making me sit in mud or high up in trees. I was frustrated with this special treatment. I wanted to be free.

Fascinated by the girl's slow, purposeful movements, I wanted to know more. I lifted my paw up and she stopped her dance, looking into my eyes. I dropped my paw, which slammed into the dirt. While momentarily stunned, she stood straight up and brought her hands around to form a circle and then slowly dropped her hands down to her side.

She plunged both arms inside her cape and they disappeared under the folds of fabric. Finally, she pulled out a box, that I later understood as plastic. The material was soft, but impermeable, unlike wood. It did not change color, nor shed the outside surface. She pushed the top of the box with a finger and the box started to make a noise that sounded like a woodpecker's "ping, ping, ping."

She stood up and looked at me with an intensity that would melt snow, but her voice was soft. The box said, "My name is Mina. What is your name?"

What is this, I wondered. Can this be real or is this my dream?

Now, this story will sound strange or just not real. But it is important to tell it just as it happened. My mind is a little tainted and it is hard for me to even remember what it was like to understand words for the first time and then use them. Words came from this plastic device and represented Mina's thought. She asked my name, which we often do when we meet other bears for the first time. I decided to try this. Oddly, when I said my name, the device did not respond. It could not speak back to Mina. It was strange, but I guess when you are in a dream, you follow the path presented to you. Words are interesting to me now, but at the time when Mina asked me my name, my name did not come out. And I tried and tried.

There was silence as I wondered what words were. She could use them and I could not.

"Well, then, I'm going to call you Pink. Are you okay with that?"

All I remember is thinking about all the things that I knew and trying to fit this situation into my history, my life. Mother and Lily called me Pink. How did she know my name? What was going to happen next? I was paralyzed in my thoughts. Were Mother and this Mina related somehow? Could she help me find Mother?

She sat down, stirred the fire, and calmly said, "Yes, I like the name Pink. Let me think of something you know, Pink." She walked around the cave and pointed to each item in the cave. "Fire." "Snow." "Ice." As the plastic device said these things, I started to understand the concept of words. It was strange. I knew these things, but I could not speak words into the plastic device.

It was a long time before I learned to use my voice, the sound that came from deep inside of my chest. Finally, I stood up and by pulling in and pushing out air from my belly, I made a sound that worked. The sound of my voice coming through the device was more than I could comprehend. My voice bounced off the walls and I noticed that Mina looked startled, but I did not smell fear from her. I sat back down. I was exhausted from the experience. I was saved by the knowledge that I was dreaming and that it was a good dream. There was no danger, so I sat and listened.

Mina went about adding to the fire. She heated the water and collected the tea for steeping. This time, the tea was hidden in another pocket of her cape. When she opened the small, folded wrapper, a deep, earthy scent reached my nose. This was special. Winter was a time when most things were drained of smell. The dream continued.

Her face shifted to a flat look, her body stood firm and motionless. I later named that look, 'purposeful.' It's a word I like to use as it reminded me of the only reason she was here. "I'm very sorry to disturb you, Pink. I know you are not used to intruders, but I need to explain my situation. It is important that you understand everything. I have a purpose." This word sent vibrations through my body when she said it.

She was ruining my long hibernation, but I still wanted to know why she was here. But, if I didn't sleep, there would be a penalty that would affect me all year.

"I have come here from a long distance and a different time. How I got here is less important than why I am here." Her voice was like spring nectar. She smelled rich, invigorating, light and gentle as her words landed against the walls of my cave. She appeared to me as a shimmery reflection rather than a real human.

The all-important tea preparation was complete. She poured the same two bowls and handed one to me and took a sip from hers. After her sip, she closed her eyes and the side of her mouth turned up. Her sapphire-blue robe shone brilliantly and her smooth dark hair framed her bone-white face. She moved, sitting directly in front of me on her knees. I was holding the bowl as before. Suddenly, she placed her hands over mine. She showed no fear as her small hands gripped my large paws. She helped, almost pushing, the bowl to my mouth. I then sipped, moving my tongue out of the way, letting the warm liquid linger in my mouth before swallowing. That was nice. I had never been close to any human before; in fact, humans took Mother away.

After we finished our tea, she put her bowl on the black mat. She placed the fan in her hands and flapped it open again, accenting the importance of the moment. I understood this now. I lay back down again, stretching my legs, motionless, listening.

CHAPTER 3

The plastic box, she called it the translator, was carefully placed on the mat in front of her. She was busy adjusting her robes to a sitting position and I was reminded of how tired I felt. I wanted to sleep without dreaming. No more. I let out a mild roar, a sound I often used with Lily when I was done with the game we were playing.

She looked frightened. Her eyes lost focus and her shoulders moved up toward her ears. She grabbed the translator, moving her mouth, directing words toward the box. "I am Mina Serono Kawaguchi. I am from Hiroshima, Japan. In 1945, a nuclear bomb was released five hundred feet from my garden. I should have died. My whole family died at the same moment. I should not be here. Sometimes I think I'm a ghost."

I clearly remember what happened next because it was the beginning of a big shift in my life. It took me a very long time to learn, speak and think words. She had to adjust as well. She repeated these six sentences, loudly, as the box spoke out, rattling the cave walls. These first words were complicated, they did not have meanings that I could not understand. As she spoke faster and louder, the words were now just noise, like a heavy rain. I was confused and angry. I lifted my paw and suddenly stood up with my claws out. She backed away, tripped on her robe as she fell over on the floor, her head just missing a rock.

Standing up slowly, with her robe filled with dirt, she pulled something that smelled like apple blossoms from her robe. That small action made me relax as I sat down, with a calm feeling starting at the tip of my nose. After each breath, my body relaxed more. I was suddenly aware that the breathing, like the apple blossoms, were slowing me down.

Standing tall and strong, I admired her bravery. I saw that before in small animals. Her robes were tangled and dangerously close to the fire as she fought to arrange herself. This moment of quieting, settling in and listening to her story surprised me. I was feeling protective of her, as I would toward Lily.

She stared at me with intense, dark eyes. She needed something from me. I finally sat down and raised my head toward her. She stared first and then slowly closed her eyes. Her voice started to flow into the air and grab my attention. She continued and I absorbed the words. Words have meaning. Each word has a meaning, like the meaning of where we were sitting was, 'Cave.' This word was the same when I stood outside and spoke the word cave. The inside word cave was the same as the outside word. Strange how one word had the same meaning for different locations. She also used one word that had many meanings. When she used the word love, she loved her garden, her husband and her baby. I was easily confused. I liked one word, one meaning. She tried to simplify her words for me. I was often confused and my head hurt.

We used the translator a lot, working on words. She said a word, pointed to an object and repeated the word-object lesson until I understood. Each time, the translator became smarter and I learned what she was saying. My curiosity was piqued and while Mina caused no threat to me, my insides spoke to me that I should be cautious. Why was she here? Finally, she opened up. I could feel her body relax as she spoke.

The following sentences sum up something important for me to understand. She said, "Pink, there is a concept called the future and the past. The future that I speak of is the year 2250. A technique called Soul Transformation was being tested, which transported souls from a catastrophic situation. We called it ST."

She could tell when I did not understand. "Let me simplify. What if a huge fire affected your woods? All creatures in the woods would burn in the fire. It would destroy everything over this big area."

That sounded terrible, but I understood and nodded.

"This device would take living beings running away from the fire and place them safely in *the other woods* at a different time of year, instead of spring, fall."

I thought about these words, 'The Other Woods.' Mina used words like future or past, but I recognized The Other Woods as something that happened differently. I already thought about Mother and what happened to her. Maybe she could live in The Other Woods, too.

"This big fire instantly burned my home, my neighbor's home, and everyone that lived there. The people from the future, the ones that created the ST device, changed my life on August 6, 1945, just before the time my home burned up. This bomb, or fire, that instantly killed all the living creatures around me, preserved me or my soul and moved me into another body." She looked up and paused, her eyes now small. "Pink, so many people died, so painfully. To show you how many people, you need to walk to the edge of the tree line and imagine an area the size of your woods. Twenty-six thousand people died inside that space. If you count all of the leaves that have fallen in that space, each leaf would represent one life."

She stopped again and sighed. I squirmed back and forth with some discomfort. I wanted to listen to her and I wanted more. My mind was crowded with so many questions. What was the future? Was the soul important to her story? What was a soul? Why was she here? How do I ask these complicated questions back to the translator? She was looking at me. Finally, I did something.

I picked up the translator and placed it on the ground in front of me. I took a deep breath. Mina sat taller and nodded. I waited, again, feeling her purpose but still could not connect to the words she used. Finally, with her help, she taught me the word, 'Repeat.' This word helped, especially when the word was not a physical object.

When she spoke about the fire, her face changed and her eyes dropped rain onto her cheek. Fire was the first word that translated in me a feeling of sadness. Fire was in my cave, but the fire she spoke about was the fire that killed, everything, trees, bushes, deer, everything. One word that had many meanings. It is the most horrible thing that can happen in the woods. All living creatures and plants would be killed and dwellings would be lost. We talked about that and my heart ached for her. The number of dead humans was equal to the number of leaves falling from trees. I could not imagine what she was saying. Are there that many humans? I was lost. Her body was stiffening as she spoke to me. This was important to her. Over time, I started to grasp which words were important and which were not. I noticed Mina took long pauses to say things. She repeated her words many times. Finally, I understood. She was going to die in a fire and the ST saved her from this painful death.

"As the fire started, ST collected my soul." She told me her soul was taken away from the garden she sat in. She said her family was left behind to die. She ended up alone, in a different body and a new place. I knew about death. When I see an animal die, I have seen something in the air, leave the body as it turns cold. Was that the soul? I started to think about this, if Mother died could her soul be captured like Mina? I was becoming interested.

Mina described in detail how this happened. She called it a flower that spins around, capturing souls. On that day, at 8:15 AM, or seconds after, her soul was captured. "Captured souls were transferred to living bodies. This became a big, big problem for the researchers. They did not know where the individual soul was transferred. They could not trace anything. They could not find the bodies where the souls landed."

I was tired. My head hurt. Mina stopped, she sighed. She got up and paced. There was a level of frustration for her and for me. She lay down and we slept. After several days of persistent communication and sleep, we had a routine. Slowly, I understood the story in small bits as she simplified. I still don't really know how I learned so many new things but I was feeling different.

Mina explained that her soul was in her new body, five years in the future, a year called 1950. She woke up in a hospital bed with only the memory of sitting in her garden, looking at the beauty of a simple maple tree.

"Living in Hiroshima was my dream. I was finally pregnant with a child. Our family had waited for this baby and his parents smiled at me in that special way. I was carrying the future. Alone in the garden that morning, I stepped out onto the *engawa* and looked onto our garden, reflecting on my good luck, *gambarou*, to have a baby we waited for during our marriage.

"To have found a home to rent with a garden and a view for my family to enjoy near the city center was a special kind of luck, almost a fluke, *kyuchu*. The luck continued when we found out I was pregnant. They wanted a boy, but I felt she was a girl. I privately named her, Saki, for hope. That morning, I set the water to boil for tea and sat down to watch the wisteria branches flow in the wind. I rose out of my chair to bend down and pick up a few leaves that fell in the garden path. The red feather-like leaves seemed strange. My maple had a beautiful, delicate leaf shape that suddenly turned yellow on the underside and then white in my hands. This strange light grew across the whole garden that surrounded me. Then everything turned white, the fence, the house, blasting away all color, everywhere.

"I looked up at the perfect tamamoto bushes, pruned into uniform oblong bubbles, which now appeared like an array of round ice globes. Strangely, at that moment, I remembered the owner of the garden and wondered if he would blame us for the whitening of the trees and shrubs. The whole garden began dissolving before my eyes, breaking apart into separate points of light and then vanishing.

"My last thought was fear. I heard voices screaming; from my husband, my mother-in-law, my neighbor? Water from the tea pot sprayed across the room. This is the last point of memory I had of my life and my former body.

"When I woke, I was confused as I looked down at my body. I lifted my arm to find my arm was longer and my nails were oval instead of square. My hair fell to my waist and was blacker and straighter. I then heard English words and people looking at me, dressed in white, with western-style hair, waves with big curls at the end. I was conscious, I was in a different body, but with a complete memory of my past. I raised the sheet and found I was no longer carrying my baby. Oh no. As fear calcified my heart, my heart started to slow down. My grief took hold of me and would not release its grip.

"While the nurses and doctors were preparing to charge me with electric shocks, I became conscious and knew I had to find my baby. I could do this! Somehow, I experienced power and worked to start my heart on my own. At that moment, I felt my body warm, from my toes to my head. I stroked my belly and felt the hope of finding my baby. That was it. Whatever strange situation I was in, I had a purpose. Saki's name was now more important because all I had was hope.

"They later told me my heart stopped, but mysteriously started on its own. As I forced myself to stay alive each day, I realized how strange it was to be in a hospital in a different body. Through a long process of looking in the mirror and down at my body, I finally understood I was younger. I looked Japanese, but no longer had the features of my mother. Whose body was this? I asked myself. No one visited me and no one communicated to me in Japanese. I knew very little about why I was there and the body that I occupied.

"Fear was inside me, a constant enemy, to the extent that I did not speak for weeks. Imagine knowing everything about my other self and having to adjust to a different body. I struggled to know what to do. I never tried to tell anyone who I really was, and I kept silent. All I could think of was Saki."

CHAPTER 4

As Mina told her story, she stopped often, helping me understand. She was calm and quiet. Her soft voice, coming through this box, created an atmosphere, fresh, blossom scent surrounding her. I listened to her words and understood she traveled a long way, looking to find her baby. That made me sad. She was a mother looking for her child and I felt like a child missing my mother.

Finally, I said it, "Mother." She nodded with her head down and eyes closed. She understood the word coming out of the box as she patted her belly. She said the word, 'Love,' back to me. Her voice startled me as it came out of the box and I felt the word. It made me sad. I was missing Mother and Lily. I wanted to tell her about what happened to them, but it was complicated. How could I put together words in a story?

She talked about love for her baby and now I had a word. This word, like a caress or nuzzle from my mother, ran up and down my spine. Whenever I heard this word, my body felt it. All these interruptions from a human, disturbing my sleep, speaking into a translator, telling me stories forced me to understand I found one interesting word. There is a word both for Mother and love. I think Mother is the sun and love is the moon.

As the tension in my throat relaxed, I looked at her and she raised her head as her face opened up, like a blue and white flower. With her small hands pressed together, she bent her willowy body deeply, as waves of her hair floated over her body.

I adjusted my posture, saying an important word. "Sleep," I said. There were more words to say, but rest was critical. We would be here in the cave, until spring. More snow fell and we needed to preserve our energy and hibernate. Food was limited and we must cool the place down and lower our metabolism. My mind was bursting and I needed to release the fullness that I felt. My next word was, 'Survival.' She bent her body over her knees, and touching the ground with her head.

She looked up, looking into my eyes and said, "I understand." This visual intensity said to me that she understood, not just the words from the box, but what was coming from me, without words. Of course, I had never had such an experience, no one, including Mother, would ever approve of being across from a human. But here I was and I needed rest.

Four winters ago, I was with Mother and Lily. In one year, both of them left me. I remember that summer, running at top speed, terrorizing any creatures who passed my way and streaking across spaces, high in the air. I raced up and down trees, never staying long in one spot. The faster I moved, the more I floated, which brought me more energy.

Mother told me humans would chase me and she also warned that other bears would shun me. She told me my color. It was pink, the same as my name. She said I was special, but would cause panic, especially with humans. She told me panic was never good. She said I needed to always, always, always stay away from humans. That, alone, would save me.

Humans were dangerous to all animal species. They did not fight with their bodies, but with a deadly tool. I studied them. They were often cruel in their killing, leaving behind gutted bodies and a smelly trail back to the road from which they came.

One time, I was sitting high in a tree on a fall day when I saw them, humans, carrying food on their backs. They spread it in piles, in the tree next to me. The food was sweet and as the smell moved into my nose, it created a desire for me to jump down and devour it. I waited for them to leave and found many similar piles of food placed around this small clearing of trees. I wanted it badly. The sweet, strong-smelling food, would add piles of weight on my bones. I would feel very happy if I had this food in my belly. Mother appeared, rushing toward the food and alerted me to move away, really fast. Had Mother not come to me, I would have started to eat right away. It was my first encounter with humans, a moment I will never forget. I can still feel the pleasure and suffering I experienced that day.

Now, after four winters, life in my world was smaller. It was a constant effort to stay away from humans. There was less wild land, more trees cut, and fewer homes for all animals. The challenge to survive sometimes kept away the loneliness I felt, alone in my cave without Mother or Lily. Survival was the only thing I had and only myself to care for. The long, cold winters kept me safe from humans. Allowing a human, this young human, into my cave worried me. Humans were my symbol for death. If I go back to hibernating, I will stop this dream and be safe again.

I was awake, my heartbeat increasing, slowly. I lifted my head to look around. There was something different as I discovered a soft breathing sound underneath me. Mina, this small human, was sleeping under my body. My blanket of fur kept her warm. She occasionally made small movements, releasing puffs of the blossoms that I remembered in my dream.

Mother established a pattern to observe this day. This day turned everything over. My heart was just a little lighter, and it lifted my spirit. Everything around me, trees and small animals and raptors, all took note. This was the day the earth turned toward the light. The change was small, the feeling was barely noticed, but it was an important moment. The turn toward the sun was slow, but the hope for spring was there. Mother described it to me. We were to honor the mid-winter shift as daylight increased each day after. It could be sunny and warm to grey and still, with cold so penetrating that even I could not stay warm.

One cannot underestimate the importance of habit on this day. I had to get up and set the ritual. I must also adjust for Mina. Mina sensed the change and crawled out from under me, a little disheveled. She was not afraid and held herself tightly as she shivered in the cold cave air that surrounded us.

This was Mother's Winter Solstice ritual. Most animals do not participate formally, but we were lucky as Mother presented us with this treat, in our first year. I added small things to the ritual after Mother disappeared. I've continued this ritual in hope I could connect with Lily, after she left me behind, following a large male bear. What is she doing right now? Does she continue this tradition?

I reached for the translator box. The following thought, passed on to me by Mother, had to be translated to words for Mina to understand. Finally, I spoke these words.

Long nights of winter

Getting shorter

Find your wild dreams

No fear

Peace and courage

Stay wild.

I felt fresh with hope as I was reminded of the memories of Mother and Lily. Lily and I heaped the fall berries and Lily drew a circle around them on the floor of the cave. She loved this part. The turning of the sun will bring us Spring and new life for plants and animals.

Mina started a small fire. She found her tea whisk and placed it next to the teapot and bowls. With such silent dignity, as if every movement was vital, she waited for the fire to turn to coals and heat the water for the tea. Holding the pot as if it was a precious stone, she stood up and poured two bowls of tea. We sat, drinking.

I finally looked at her face and neck. Her pale pink skin offsetting her jet-black hair with a streak of white dividing her face in half, created a peculiar impression that she was perfectly balanced with everything she did.

After the warm tea, my body temperature turned up. We piled the berries high and I reached for a branch, trying to draw a circle around them. It was not Lily's round, perfect object. I was too big to move like her. Mina understood and smoothed away the circle I scratched out. Her concentration was the same as when she made tea. She moved her head toward the ground and walked backwards. This circle was perfect. Lily would have loved this!

"Why are we here?" Mina spoke into the translator for the first time since we awakened. I did not understand this. What kind of question is this? She picked up the bowls, stored the few remaining berries and moved into her cozy location for more sleep. I was surprised and delighted at that. She got it! This time of awakening was meant to be brief. Metabolic rates were slowing and we would enter into sleep until the winter was over. Why are we here? What does that mean? And that is all I remembered about the Winter Solstice I spent with Mina.

CHAPTER 5

I woke up, noticing that Mina was again, tucked next to my belly, the warmest spot in the cave. She carved out a hollowed cocoon in the dirt with a long piece of fabric protecting the space above and below her small body. I felt like we were in the forest when my heart is quiet and nature whispers in my ear. This small graceful human was with me and I felt full, like with Mother and my new word, 'love'. I tried not to move, but my body had a different idea. I immediately started to think about what she asked during the winter solstice. The question she asked, why are we here? Questions like this are strange. I've never asked a question using why. I ask what is this tree? Does it have branches close to the ground to make climbing easier? I ask are there fish in the stream behind the rocks that cause water to become noisy. I have never asked why the rocks are here. I have never asked why spring is green and fall brown. Each time I used this new word, 'why', my mind stopped. I would much prefer to ask, 'where are the fish' not 'why are there fish'.

As my heart beat faster, my body heat warmed the cave. Mina started to move. Her blue-black eyelashes opened up next to my face, revealing deep, dark eye pools. With her hair black as night, softly tangled, she pushed herself to an erect position. She first turned her head, then her neck and then her spine in one direction and then the other, like an owl surveying the cave for creatures. She looked aware, as if there was a lot going on in the cave. What a delicate creature, like a flower. I sighed, blowing more warm air into the cave.

Slowly light moved into the cave, until its brightness reflected through the melting snow covering the entrance, casting sparkles of light against the walls. Sounds of birds filtered through the ice glass. Birds returning, waking up to a fresh new day. With the added light warming the cave and the temperature rising, I started to stretch my legs and arms, filling the cave with my body. Mina moved around me, dodging my movements.

This moment of contrast, comparing my pinkish bulk to this pale rose-colored, lady-slipper, would be fixed in my memory, never to change. However, the business, the business of living must take place. This never-ending stream of things one must do to survive is a different set of actions, especially when you are pink.

Each year was different, and today, I was filled with excitement as my body followed a bright, fresh sensation warming my heart. Waking with Mina, a companion, was giving me unique energy. I pushed my head through the sparkling door of light, reducing the crystalized snow covering the door to tiny little light-balls spreading across the floor of the cave. Fresh, cool air pummeled into the cave. I started speaking without the translator. Mina pulled it out of her pocket. She caught the end of my speech with, "If I was not so hungry, I would think this is the best time of year." I moved out with unusual agility.

There were things to observe. The snow was softening. If you were a burrowing animal, your precious little passage under the snow would collapse. It was a tough time for them since the ground was still frozen and the only alternative was to walk on top of the snow, sinking often. Each year would present different challenges for small creatures, depending on the amount of snow, the temperature coming from light and time since the last snowfall. Large creatures, like bears, were also challenged but it was the little creatures I had a warm feeling for.

As I walked, Mina followed, moving through the soft snow behind my large path. I pushed through the snow with ease. The birds had a lot to say, unencumbered. The fresh, crisp air was silent, the sounds of tree buds pushing out, all excellent signs of a hopeful year. Saki was Mina's word for hope.

I looked down and noticed Mina's head staring down. Footprints! The prints were larger than hers and fresh. The snow had not melted and the edges were crisp and deep. This was the print of a human. I started to track the boot prints, as Mina followed behind me, struggling to keep up. The path became steep, going up a hill and stopping just above the cave entrance. Rocks crowned the hill with a body, planted face down in the snow next to the largest stone. Mina cried out with a high-pitched noise. I noticed Mina had water dripping down her robes. As I moved slowly toward the body, I saw it was a man. Based on the smell, it was not dead, but the heart was slow, as if in hibernation. We both stared quietly. I had no fear and Mina did not speak.

He was a tall, wiry, wrinkled man, with thinning hair, a long jacket and pants that had a slight stretch, making the pants appear tailored and pressed. His boots were hard leather, but softened with age and wear. Mina bent down and lifted his face out of the snow and turned his body over. She touched his face gently. Steam was rising from his body, still warm. He might have fallen over the ice-covered rocks and knocked himself out. He was breathing slowly. Mina spoke words, but he did not respond. She motioned me to move him, bending down and placing her arms underneath his waist. She tried, but could not lift the body. I did not need a translator to know what she wanted.

This man was human. No matter how thin and non-threatening he seemed, I could not help save him. He looked more like a large, long-legged insect than any man I had seen. Mina then picked up his legs and dragged him down the hill. Mina had a strange power over me. She stared at me, legs apart and hands on her hips. I understood and placed the man in my mouth. His body almost floated in air as I walked back to the cave and dropped him onto the cave floor. Mina started a fire, arranged a spot for him close to the warm air and started to boil water for tea. She looked through her bags and pulled out a very small indigo-colored bag. She pulled out a mixture of leaves that had a pungent smell, a new smell to me.

She brought out the translator. "This is a special tea for injury which has an antibiotic effect, and a sleep inducer. I think this might help, but I'm not sure." He needed her medicine to stay alive. Why is this happening? This human did smell different from others. He smelled more like the wet leaves of fall from the forest bottom and his clothing matched the color of pine tree needles. Now I had two humans in my cave.

When the water was almost boiling, the small, thin man rolled from his back to face the fire, like a plant turning toward the sun. Mina smiled ever so slightly. She sat down and stroked the man's head, making his hair all point in the same direction.

"I've seen a man like this before, in picture books about Germany. They wore green costumes like this with wool socks in beautiful colors of teal, red and thin lines of yellow. These thick socks probably saved this man's life."

She took off his shoes and socks, rubbing his feet. The man remained motionless. He just stared at the fire. She pulled out a large hunting knife, complete with a jagged edge that could be used for dressing a deer or scaling a fish. I shuddered. The thought of bringing this human into my cave was building in me. Why did I allow this to happen? Mina opened up his knapsack, stared into it and then looked up at me, surprised. She called it a newspaper. I could not accept any of this and I left the cave.

CHAPTER 6

I watched Mother kill a human. After we ran back from the piles of sticky, sweet food, Mother told us to stay in the cave until she returned. We sat in the cave, waiting for a long time. Lily started to cry out in hunger. I left the cave, looking for Mother. I followed her scent, and finally heard sounds. Mother was running toward a human, bolting as fast as I ever saw her run. I then sensed the human smell of fear. Mother slowed down as she saw me approach, turned and knocked him down with the force of her weight. She stood over him, pinning him with her paws. She took two bites from his arm that fit between her teeth perfectly. She then snapped his head which caused his eyes to change to white and his body to go limp. She then tossed the body in the air and it dropped down right in front of me. I did not move, but took in all of the smells of a human. We left quickly, back to the cave, leaving the dead human behind.

After that, we were very careful, completely avoiding human contact. If we encountered human scent or that strange sweet smell, we were gone. Once we noticed signs of humans coming closer to our birth cave, we moved far away, to this cave-of-safety. This woods never had human smells up until now. Now I have two humans in my cave.

Was Mina going to be safe with the human, alone? I listened to the sounds of Spring, as my heart slowed down. I sat for a moment and then roamed around to find dried red bush berries. Things in my mind were now quiet. I even asked myself the question Mina asked. Why are you here? Thanks to Mina, I had new ideas and words to ask questions. One thing was clear, I needed to kill the human. That is what Mother would say. Safety from humans was my purpose.

I returned to the cave and found that Mina took off one robe to warm this human. She placed the translator between us and asked me if I was okay. Okay. I heard the word and understood the meaning. It was not what I was feeling. It was against my nature to not kill him now and Mina looked like she knew that without the translator. As the day wore on, Mina sat, watched, staying close to his limp body. His face was calm and peaceful. When Mina leaves the cave, I will kill him.

Mina was sleeping as I watched the man stand, his head almost touched the cave ceiling. He first looked down at her and then at me in the corner. I stood up, fully occupying the cave space with my hair standing up, pushing this man toward the corner, away from the cave entrance. He was weak and shaken. I moved closer and smelled him up close. His woodsy smell reminded me of fall. Why was he here? What would Mother do? He was broken; a small, old, frail, sick man. I could let him stay for now. There would be no challenge in breaking his neck.

Mina woke instantly, jumped up and was shouting as I stood over the man. Without the translator between us, I knew what she was saying. She was a human protecting her species. I was in a position of strength. I looked at him more carefully. His facial hair was curly gray, unlike hair I saw before. His spiky thin hair and soft clothing, combined with green pants were like moss. He was like an old fox I saw one time, too tired to hunt. He then sat down, trembling.

I left the cave and then came back. Establishing dominance was important, but I didn't need to kill him right now. Mother told me never to let any human live that saw me. Now I had two humans that saw me. I had to think about that. Taking action would be easier than working on my new question, why are humans in my cave? Killing him would upset Mina and my new purpose was to take care of her, like taking care Lily. I had to think about their smells. They did not smell like the threat of Mother's humans. Could they be different? I wish Mother was here to decide.

The human was now inspecting the corners and looking around in panic. He was moving about without shoes. Humans needed shoes so he was not going to leave quickly. Mina stood, only as tall as his lower rib cage, and looked up. She motioned for him to sit down next to the fire. Her graceful white hand took his and tugged on him to sit. After a few pulls, he sat. His angular figure was not flexible as he crossed his legs like an insect. She handed him the translator. She spoke into it and said, "Hello, I am Mina. How are you feeling?"

The surprise created a funny eye-popping look on the man's face. He stood up, absorbed in staring and turning the translator around in his hands. In response to her question, he spoke back and said, "I'm in pain."

The way he spoke compared to Mina was quicker, firm and still soft. Talking back and forth was complicated. Mina quickly exchanged a lot of words with him, she nodded and asked, "You are speaking Austrian?"

"Yes," he said.

For now, I accepted the situation. He was not an immediate threat. I moved across the outside opening to listen, knowing he was not going to leave.

She sat down in her graceful way and relaxed her shoulders. She moved her hands in the air from me to him. She picked up the translator and set it next to him, sitting for a long time without speaking. Sitting in quiet was a relief, but I remembered her question, why are you here, during the solstice. I thought about what to do and what words to use. I grabbed the translator and said, "Why are you here?" My voice was loud and was repeated as the words hit against the walls of the cave.

The human jumped, but Mina grabbed his waist and pulled him down to sit. He resisted and she then held him down with force by gripping his shoulders, and putting her head in front of his face. What a sight, seeing her tiny body, facing down this man. She grabbed the translator from him and placed it in his hands. He looked down at it and said nothing for a long time. When he began speaking, it was a soft, bird-like voice with a nice regular lilt to it. He opened with:

"I am from Austria, my name is Claudius. I am a killer. I killed millions of humans."

Mina raised her hand to stop his talking. She looked at me with an open face. She asked me if I understood him. I told her it was hard and she repeated over and over that she would help me understand. As words came out, Mina asked for a pause and helped me understand. I was curious, not tired anymore. By the time it was over, I understood enough to know that this man was okay. Not good like Mina was good, but he talked about love and I had strong feelings about that word. The following is a summary of what Claudius said, using this long tiresome process of Claudius to Mina and Mina to me.

"I was born in 1860 in Spital, Gmünd, of Lower Austria. This small village, of only 150 people, was where I went to school. My home was surrounded by tall native trees and the view out of each window was more beautiful than the other. The majestic castle stood high on the hill, too beautiful to be real and I felt like I was living in a storybook. The air was clean and crisp. Small villages like ours were sprinkled across the land, tucked into their own domains. We called them sheltered little hamlets. My parents were simple and thrilled to have one son that they could care for and dote on in an almost crushing way that made me feel lonely. When I turned ten, I discovered I could walk long distances, hike through the woods, using convenient trails that crisscrossed the valley. I was a happy boy. Once I hiked in the beauty of the mountains and the forests, I no longer felt lonely. My heart lifted each time I walked and, over the years, I became a hiker, walker, and an expert skier from the most famous mountain range in the world. I was a traveler with a wonderful home base and parents that loved and supported me in my many trips, sometimes very long.

Everywhere I went, I found things that burst my heart, filled my soul with rich textures of beauty and peace. These were the best days of my life. Little did I know what would happen to me."

From time to time, Mina paused to answer my questions. I was especially interested in his expression, "burst my heart." I also understood the feeling when my heart physically caught up to things around me that made me happy. That expression combined perfect words that named my feelings about being happy. I often felt that way when I played with Lily in the creek.

"I entered school at six and excelled in math, physics but loved language and music. Teaching methods were for the average student. There were no advanced studies for my unique skills and my teacher did not reach out for a solution either. I continued to take long walks. Once I discovered train tracks, it was easier to walk toward the Alps at a faster and easier pace. These tracks were connected to more towns, and I could visit their worlds. Homes lining the tracks were nicely organized, perfectly maintained, as detailed as puzzle pieces. Kale, lettuce, and fruit trees were everywhere, which was typical of an Austrian diet. I would occasionally just drop down for a tomato or an apple as I continued my trips. I adopted this life and would have been happy, except for one thing.

"She was the love of my life. When you love someone before puberty, it is a rich and soulful relationship, built on innocence, authenticity and loyalty. I did not have to act a certain way or hide anything. We were friends and shared everything. I showed her places of beauty, moss in the forest floor that collected sunlight at a certain time of day. The forest floor was so soft and squishy to walk on that we took off our shoes and walked all over the moss patches. She delighted in this. She said its translucent beauty gave her a feeling of God's presence. Her parents insisted that she stay close to her home, but there were still wonderful things to show her that did not require long walks. The rest of my life is blurry compared to the precious moments I spent with her. Nothing was erased, even with my aging memory. I think about it like one remembers a dream that woke you up in the middle of the night, so pleasant, that you just wanted to stay sleeping.

"Klara was raised by hard-working, conservative, der bauer, peasants. Her parents raised her to be obedient. Klara was my age, we shared everything. She had many household tasks to complete. I always found an excuse to come and help her when I could. Her parents were not friendly, and I was never invited in for dinner. When Klara turned 16, she suddenly became sullen. I was not sure what was going on. She stopped attending school. One day I went to her home and was told she moved to Braunau. Her mother told me she started a new job. My heart clenched; it was all I could do to breathe."

Claudius stopped to look at Mina and then to me. His face changed when he said, "My heart felt tight and my lungs would not fill up with air. My parents called it asthma but I knew that my illness was from my heart ache for Klara." I felt him at this point. No words were needed. I know this was my experience when Mother disappeared.

"I should have gone right away to Braunau to get her to come back to me or know that I missed her. Later, I heard she was to be a servant for someone close to the family, her second cousin. This was my chance to save her and bring her home. I did nothing. I was so certain that we were going to be together, I was sure something like fate would intervene. I was depressed. I could not sleep nor eat and I stayed in my room instead of hiking. Finally, my mother intervened and sent me away to the Italian Alps. And that was it. My biggest mistake of my life, but not just my life, the lives of a million of other human beings. Why didn't I go to Klara and tell her how I felt about her?"

The human looked down into the fire and then, with a deep sigh, said, "I destroyed the world with my lack of courage. My ineptitude, my lack of strength, everything I did was incompetent, I was a complete idiot, but how was I to understand the implications beyond myself and my life? I thought Klara deserved to marry someone stronger, quicker, richer than myself. She needed financial support in order to have lots of children. Children that could be properly educated, go to the proper schools and have big families themselves. She could sit with her grandchildren in old age and know she provided everything she could to make them grow strong and healthy. And I knew I was not capable of providing that kind of family support. The kind of love I had was the kind that thought this way. I was doing what was right for Klara and I should not be a part of that picture. I messed it up. I was supposed to tell Klara I loved her and it was fear that held me back."

CHAPTER 7

There was a break in the clouds and the light streamed into the cave with a reflection bouncing against the limestone walls. Mina adjusted her wrap. The human seemed to notice this change in the light. He looked up, smiled and then looked tired. His tall body sank down while his head was held erect. Mina motioned him to lie down. Exhaustion had covered his face with pain. He had long lines starting at his cheekbones in a vertical line, almost as if they were scars from a fight. His body slowly relaxed and he immediately dropped into sleep. Mina got up, grabbed the translator and walked around me to get outside the cave. I followed her as I lifted my nose filling it with the smell of spring. She took frequent, long deep breaths.

Finally, she spoke, "I was so caught up in his story, I never asked his age. He said he was born in 1860 and was directed here, to these woods. He is 90 years old. I can relate to his deep sorrow. Maybe I know why he is here but I have to think about this. The newspaper in his bag is from North Carolina. That is the exact location I came from."

We walked to the stream and sat down together. We both looked around at the stream. This river-let always brought me peace and I could see she was quiet too. As I studied her face, she was taking in the beauty of nature, the sounds of birds and the sparkle of the sun through the moisture from the melted snow. She looked calm, comfortable, sitting quietly, saying nothing.

I understood her and felt close to her, like I felt toward Lily. She now framed a new question for me. Why were Claudius and Mina here? Was there a purpose? I was beginning to understand time travel. It was five years since that day she stared into her garden, looking at her beloved maple tree. Why was she looking for her baby here?

"Pink, I'm at the end of my journey. Claudius may be an important piece to finding my baby. Let's create a safe place and nurture him back to health. I need you to help me do that."

As Mina shared her thoughts, mine also churned around in my head. "Let's go back to our question. Why are you here? Why is he here? I'm a bear, I know why I'm here. For me to be with humans is unnatural and dangerous. I have a concern."

"Okay," she said. "I'll show you why I'm here."

I followed her to a large open space of white, surrounded by slivers of water advancing toward the center from the shore. This was how my lake thawed in the spring, from the shore out toward the center. Close to her was a large flat stone peeking through the snow. Smaller stones lined up perfectly from the shore, as if a path was formed to it. She carefully stepped on the smallest stone, avoiding puddles and mud, and nimbly found her way to the largest stone. She reached into her robe and pulled out a blue object, an orb, raising it up toward the sun. She then placed it on the large flat stone. There were waves of blue beams surrounding the object. A large, band of birds were flying from across the lake, toward her, creating a dark shadow as they cut out rays of the sun. As the birds passed over her, she covered her body with her robes and waited until the sun shown again. She sat down, arranging herself and melting her body onto the stone. My eyes only looked at her as she reflected each beam of light that came down to her. A warm wind changed directions, the ice melted around the stone, and a strong vibrating energy radiated from the orb. My body sensed, 'Something was going to happen.'

Mina's form was shifting. Her belly moved slowly, pushing out a round shape, forming a large impression outside the blue robe. She was forced to stand up as the berries she had eaten earlier, came back up out of her mouth. Just moments before, she was small and now her body was expanding as if she swallowed a squirming snake. She started to remove her robes. Once the outer garments were removed, she was naked, except for a thin sheath of fabric. She started to shake from the cold. What was happening? Can I help? As if she heard, she shook her head.

As her body moved back and forth, her stomach stretched almost to the size of the rock she sat on. The cloth became soaked as sweat came out of her body. Finally, she screamed for help. I ran to pick her up and take her to shore onto the soft snow. She gasped for air as I laid her down, staring forward with that purposeful expression.

Her facial expression was angular and red. I looked at her slight body and small white stature, blending into the snowy landscape. She was shaking and showing signs of struggle. Then she closed her eyes. I was worried and concerned about how to help her. Her body continued to change as if the snake turned into a bulging otter, with a big fleshy belly. Her body expanded even more. She was going to break the flesh surrounding this bump. She was pregnant with a baby wanting to come out. I did not understand this at the time, I never saw a human up close like this and not one that was pregnant. I was shaken. I did not believe this was happening. Common sense took over, and I stayed close to her. I selected the largest piece of cloth and laid it across her body. The beautiful sapphire-blue, with small gold flecks reflected against the sunlight, made her look like a queen bee in full blush. I was stunned by her brilliance and the overall spectacle of her new body shape. Finally, the convulsions stopped and her muscles relaxed. She faced the sky, watching the blue sky above, as her body collapsed, emptied of the shape that was inside.

As if waiting for her to die, the birds returned, passing over us, casting the black shadow of nighttime. It was colder and darker than before, but she slept as I waited. I didn't know how long she would rest, hopefully she would awaken before night time. I wondered if I should wake her and bring her back to the cave. I thought about how unlucky this day was. Could I handle this? Could I take care of her?

Later, she told me, "The pain was strange, like I was a passive observer of what was happening to my body. I was fearful of what was going to happen next. The last thing I thought about was my Japanese garden, the stone and the tree, and the small fountain that my father-in-law gave me when we were married. I thought about the flash of the atomic bomb, and then blanked out. This was too sad a memory for me."

As I waited for her to waken, I noticed the chatter of the birds and the loons on the lake calling back and forth to each other. There was no sign of the dark band of flying birds.

She finally woke up, laying against my fur, with her head supported by my leg. Her eyes, black as a moonless night, looked at me with sadness. Her body was lost inside the robes. Nothing moved. She spoke clearly. "Where is the Orb?"

I knew what she was asking and handed it to her as it quickly disappeared inside her robes.

"I'm looking for my child. This has happened before. I'm pregnant, I go through labor, I fall asleep and then I'm awake, without my baby. You saw me. I cannot bring her back. The stone holds magic that will help me find Saki. Dr. N told me to practice until I get it right. I'm on a long journey that brought me here, to this place, Pink. But I think something has changed and that has to do with Claudius. We need to think about Claudius and why he is here."

I nodded without hearing all of her words. I remembered what I saw and felt her strong desire to find her baby. Her purpose. She reminded me of spring, as dead things come up green, with bright smells and delicate textures.

She lay there, depleted, no energy to even to move a finger or a toe. Looking up with soft eyes, she asked, "Tell me about life with your mother, Pink."

I told her about warm spring days when all the creatures moved toward light and the warmth of the sun.

"Could you hear tree buds pop open?" she asked.

"Yes, you could, but you could hear so much more. Everything was alive and everything that could speak did, which developed into this mixture of music and sounds, all singing together. It was our first year when Mother finally let us go outside the cave. I stopped to look around, my nose was filled and I saw trees for the first time. Everything stunned me. The small, dark, warm cave was replaced with a blue sky, woody trees, and miles and miles of ground to walk.

"Lily and I played together that first day. We did not stop running, jumping off tree stumps, and rolling. We tumbled with each other; so happy to have space to move and muscle to stretch. Mother watched and seemed worried, always reminding us to look around. She worried about deep holes we could fall into or snakes we could roll on. She was worried, but we played and stayed close enough to feed from time to time. That was always nice. After that first day of play, Mother would take us through the woods, foraging for food and drinking water from the creek. We stayed close and rarely did Mother leave us alone.

"I remember noticing a difference between me and my sister or, rather, how differently Mother treated us. Lily was a dark brown. She vanished against the dark brown trees we climbed. At night, she was even darker, but I could always sense her as she was noisy in her movements. I could smell her too. Mother would sometimes give a signal to hide and she would become still and blend into the woods. I would do the same, but Mother was always nervous about me and in any dangerous situation, she would run and quickly cover me with her body. I was bothered with this game and quickly joined Lily when it was over. My coat was different, a bright color, almost matching the color of Mother's mouth when she opened it wide to yawn. My color was a constant concern to Mother.

"One day, a timber wolf observed us. We were still pretty young, and Mother had left us to seek fish in the stream. We were vigorous in our play and I did not smell things like I do now. Wolves are masters of disguise. I know the smell now and how they quickly move in packs of three or more. This wolf might have been thinking two young bears would feed his family. Mother was too far away to know about the wolf. His sudden appearance froze us. The smell was a combination of dead flesh and hair when it is wet. The smell itself was very powerful and we instantly knew what danger smelled like. Mother called this, "the carnivore smell".

"What happened next surprised me. Lily made loud warning noises for Mother to hear. I stood up on two legs, arching my back and walked toward the wolf, while balancing my arms forward. The wolf was obviously very stunned by this movement as he sat there, stared and did not attack. My forward motion pushed him backward, as he turned and ran away. I looked back at Lily and she was still crying out. Mother came back and raised her nose to smell what happened. There were lots of signs that something was wrong and she quickly assessed the situation based on the smell of the excrement left behind. She later named me, "Pink Bear Scared Big Wolf," but it was always Pink for short.

She often stared at me for long periods and started new training for us to practice. That included walking on two legs. That night, we came together in a tight ball, feeding on Mother and feeling excited about learning new skills. Mother said she would give us useful tools that we will need in the future."

I could tell Mina liked the story. I did not have to stop and help her understand. She smiled and was relaxed. "How old are you, Pink?"

"It can be measured by the winter solstice. Mother said we were born that day. I've completed four rituals, three on my own." Once the translator completed my language, her mouth turned up and her face brightened.

"Tell me more about Mother." She relaxed with her face fixed only on me.

The translator was still hard to work, but I took my time and continued.

"After the wolf incident, Mother selected a portion of the northern woods that was rarely traveled by humans. The density of these woods made it difficult for travel and escape, even for deer. There were no roads, no tree-cutting, no signs of humans at all. The natural remoteness of this area kept it safe for us. This small creek and tiny lake were so isolated, we did not see signs of humans. A few moose walked through and the wolves left us alone. We were in the best place to isolate from the biggest predator, humans.

"One time, Mother took us into the center of the creek. I swam down to a deep hole and bit into a large, snakelike fish. As the fish thrashed around, I bit deeper into the scaly body. As I came to the surface, the fish started to lose energy. By the time I reached the banks of the creek, my fish was quiet. Mother came over, pleased and proud. Lily and I immediately feasted, tearing apart the large fish. Mother showed us how to bite down on big bones, before we swallowed.

I helped Lily to learn to catch fish and later, she was faster than I was. After feasting, we walked slowly back to the cave and lay down to sleep. That was an important day for me. We both had good skills.

"I was getting big and could not hide behind Mother. If I spent time in the water where only my head showed, I was safe. I could also walk out of the water on my two legs and frighten anything in my way. But, something about my color was out of place even in this woods and I started to feel strange. Mother was worried, but she still encouraged me to be strong and she wanted to teach me to kill things besides fish. She said it was not just about me, but protecting Lily. I already knew that.

"My sister was not aware of my struggle. She did not see I was different. She knew I was different from Mother, but she did not understand why my color was odd. She was my constant companion. We fished and looked for food together all summer long.

"In that first year, as the summer's warmth passed, Mother would be gone for longer periods of time. When she returned, we waited for her stories even before we took her milk. Her stories of many lakes, lots of fish, muddy patches and little minnows made us happy. We listened quietly. Her voice soothed us and helped us sleep quickly. The sun was always a topic of great curiosity. Why did it look yellow sometimes and sometimes was red, close to the ground? Why did it bring us warmth like a fire does but not during hibernation? Why did it move in the sky around us? It was unlike anything else. I now realized that I used 'Why' words also.

"With her stories, she told us details about hunting, fishing and finding berries. Climbing trees was a critical part of her education. This was only a protective move, but also could be used in defense. As we got higher in a tree, we could see across many acres of land and look for danger. We knew danger and I love reaching the tops of trees.

"Our trees were tall, straight, with many, many branches. While they were big, the wind still pushed them back and forth while we held tight. My weight could bend a tree branch, but not the whole tree. There were three kinds of wind. Light wind that passed through the underbrush of the woods, a stronger wind that moved midway up the trees and those big, dangerous ones that forced big trees to creak loudly and sometimes break. When that happened, climbing trees was not a good idea, no matter what the danger.

"When Mother left us, we were sensitive to all movements around us. We could smell dangerous situations and raced back to the cave as she told us to do. I feel anxious now, just thinking about that time, knowing we were often wild and reckless, sometimes not following Mother's rules. She cautioned us to even avoid other bears, especially male ones. If hungry enough, she said they might eat us. We focused on routines and found that play gave us new learnings. We clawed fiercely at each other, pushed off each other's backs and flew into brush and small trees. Each time a new game was developed, a new skill became important, and we preened with excitement when Mother returned. She was cautious with her praise, always worried about what bad things could happen to us. Lily had a gentle sweetness about her, but once she felt threatened, in play, she turned into a fierce, scary tall bear with a big open mouth. Her claws came out easily, as she mauled fictitious creatures, one by one. Our growing confidence gave us the belief we could conquer anything. This really worried Mother. She always said, not yet, you are not ready.

"It happened later in the fall when leaves fell from the trees, the time when you could see far into the woods."

At this point of the story, Mina asked me, "This is the bad part of the story, Pink, right?"

I sat back, amazed that Mina, a human, could sense this right away. "Bad? Is there a stronger word for it? Maybe, but it changed my life forever. Lily and I spent the day fishing and drinking from the fresh creek, challenging each other to look for small fish and sucking up schools with our mouths. This took more time than catching bigger fish, but it was fun and the competition was fierce. After this semi-successful fishing day, we lay down together, forming a brown and pink ball. We felt the day cool quickly. As we waited for Mother to return and to share our new game with her, the sun set. Lily made a quiet whimper that expressed what I was feeling. Where was Mother? She always returned before it was dark. Why isn't she back? We curled up even closer, matching the warmth of Mother. We slept well, but awoke sad and scared.

"The next morning, we waited. We did not play or eat, but just observed the trees swaying and listened to the breeze for unusual sounds. Sometimes birds could be helpful, alerting with a kind of song that provided a warning. But that day, the woods were strangely silent. All we could hear was the sound of wooden branches clacking, touching each other, moving without the cushion of leaves. This swaying and clacking, made strong, irritating noises. We became increasingly uneasy. We were worried, like Mother worried. After listening for a while, we thought about everything that Mother said. She said she would always return to us. She also told us never to go beyond the creek, never cross the creek to the other side and never go very far from the distance between the creek and the cave. She said she needed us to always stay here so she could find us when she came back. She never told us what to do if she didn't return. Maybe she found 'danger' and needed our help.

"We both climbed the tall trees, looking out for Mother and for danger. We did not see anything. Lily said she could find Mother by following her smell, her greatest skill. She would need our help when we found her. Going against her instruction, we set out to follow her marks and her musk. We roamed all day and followed what was her freshest scent. We were excited and a little careless. As the smell became stronger, Lily noticed a human smell coming from the one direction we never traveled. Her scent became strange. It was mixed with fear, which we rarely smelled on Mother. Her strong smell continued and the human smell also became stronger. Then the smell of defecation filled our noses. Lily stopped first and I slowed down. We both rose to our feet, noses in the air, Mother was close. Lily shook her head and moved slowly. Caution was the word. Where was the human and where was Mother? We came into a clearing and saw nothing.

"We went crazy and raced back and forth around the circle, sniffing and raising our noses to understand where she was. This confusion filled our heads. She was here, but her scent had changed. Where was she? Was she hurt? We each climbed a tree and looked down. I was certain something was wrong. I then noticed a trail leading to a pool of guts and blood. Around the blood, was grass pressed down and large foot prints from two humans. How did we miss that? Lily started to cry, and I cried too. We could not remember anything after that. We cried and Lily almost fell off the tree. We found branches to sit on and sat down to wonder where Mother was. The night was still and we listened without sleeping. Animals, maybe mice and raccoons, rustled leaves and branches below us. We called back and forth, stranded, abandoned and completely stunned by what was happening. Once we could see the sun rise above the horizon, we got down. Once we got to the ground, we chanted, "Mother, Mother, Mother." Nothing, no answer, just a quiet wood. We circled one last time and knew it was bad to stay. We started back to our cave. Our hearts pounding as we took each step, a heavy burden invaded our whole bodies. Each step was painful from the inside. The birds started their chorus again, but songs no longer brought joy. We suffered heartbreak, like you did, Mina, but we did not even know what that was. We were injured, everything hurt, starting from each step we took away from Mother's scent. Our pace was slow and careless, not knowing where we were going, but we knew the general direction of home. With each movement, our tired bodies sent a signal of pain to our brains. It was unbearable. Once we returned to the creek, we went directly to the cave, excited that Mother might be waiting. Except for her smell, she was not there.

Exhaustion was so great that we got into a big ball and fell into a deep sleep.

"The next day, Lily sobbed a lot. She was lonely and her body shook with pain. I also shook, but deep inside my brain, I processed information about the circle of trees, the human smell and the blood. I was mixed up and confused and sad, as sad as Lily when she sobbed and cried out for Mother.

"I needed something stable to hold. I needed to clear my mind. While Lily slept, I sat, listened, and used all of my senses to understand. I felt some relief and continued to sit and clear my mind. Doing nothing helped take away my body's misery in losing Mother.

"We stayed in the cave for several days, Lily weeping and sleeping with no motivation to move at all and me sitting and calming myself. We were dehydrated, and Lily finally got up to leave the cave for water. We slowly made our way to the creek. We could hear the familiar sound of the rapids and the fresh smell they generated, pushing water into the air and creating wonderful moisture banks of humidity."

"Let's go back," said Lily.

"We went to the circle of trees and Lily found Mother's scent again. We noticed things we missed before. Bravely, we walked up to the pile of guts and blood but were confused by the unfamiliar smell. There were tracks and broken branches going in one direction, away from our woods. There were two types of human smells and both disappeared quickly beyond the circle. We did not stay as the human smell was overwhelming and dangerous."

I stopped and looked at the translator in wonder. How could this box tell my story to Mina? I was feeling calm, as if I was with my sister again. Lily and I always knew what each other was thinking and this device was doing the same thing with Mina. I realized my relief had to do with the translator. I felt Mother was with me when I used words about her.

Mina repeated these words several times. "I understand, Pink,"

Mother warned us about hunters. She shared in detail the many ways hunters kill bears. Mother told us many things about what could happen, including metal traps with food around them, holes in the ground covered with tree branches, killing with bullets and poisoned food. Something happened to her and we did not know what that was. Would I ever know what happened? I thought about how everything changed after that day.

"Lily and I talked about what Mother would do if a human found her. Would she walk away from our cave, like a bird mimicking a broken wing?

"After her disappearance, we taught ourselves many things about being cautious and careful about where and when we traveled. Losing Mother saved us. Each skill learned gave us another piece of information that would save our lives. When we looked for food, we always moved into areas having no human smells. This was absolute protection. All of Mother's lessons came back to us. She spent her life helping us and she was still guiding us in our heads. When I thought about her, Lily's eyes would flow with salty water. The connection of having this thought, then silently communicating to each other, was strong. Each day, we knew our relationship was key to survival.

"I started to travel on my own more, but always returned to my sister. I measured how far human smell was from our cave. In my wanderings, I rarely smelled humans, but from time to time, there were foot prints on the road that were new.

"When we wandered for food, I created a magic circle around us. If a human crossed that line, we moved. It was a simple solution. The woods protected us. We understood the many signs and paid attention to everything. Birds were helpful, but it took a lot of patience to understand their songs. Lily was good at that, too. Her excellent hearing and acute sense of smell gave us the extra protection we needed. While these patterns continued, Mother's presence faded. We became established with our own routines. We were accomplished.

"Looking back on that year, the memories of our youthful games with Mother were still strong, but the days after her absence were stiffened with sadness. I tried to protect Lily by acting like Mother, but she ignored me. Our power was in being together and equal. Lily was clear that she could handle each situation by herself. We thought about Mother less and less. By the time Lily left me, I was strong and understood that she was following Mother's path. She found a mate and suddenly moved away."

As Mina listened quietly, I realized that she reminded me of Lily. I was happy, just sitting here remembering those months with Lily after Mother died. I wondered what Lily was doing with her mate. Did she have baby bears?

CHAPTER 8

Resting after my long story, Mina curled up and fell asleep. She lay quietly with no sound coming from her mouth. I did not know what to think about her body changing on that rock.

I looked around, listened to the familiar 'watchers' that gave alerts long before anything invaded our space. As I listened, I was reminded how each season had a different sound. With Spring, the migrating birds showed up, singing their songs of attraction. The dance for attention on full display, getting busy with plans to procreate. My cave was located in a major migration route, established years ago. This area provided the protection of woods and an expansive waterway. One bird that I noticed over the years had a clear voice, ranging several octaves, whose songs lifted me up.

A bird sat on a branch above us, this one was always the first to arrive. It stayed only a few days each year, as it moved north. It was this bird's song that woke Mina up. She raised her head, looked around and spotted the blue bird, showing off with her special music and bright color. Mina smiled, showing no evidence of stress. She sat and smiled until the bird flew away. With the concert ending, she blinked and stared at me. She was composed, looking like a white flower, beautiful to just stare at. She bunched up her many cloths that wrapped her body and stood up.

I wanted to show Mina the creek. I motioned to her and we followed the edge of the lake. We walked up a small hill and could hear the water splashing before we saw it. These water sounds opened up her eyes, she gathered her cloths and bounced down the hill. The sun was now burning with warmth as the remainder of the snow melted.

"The water looks refreshing, clean and safe. I'm going in the creek." Without a lot of hesitation, she unwound her clothes, leaving the gauzy covering on. She easily found a small pool and jumped in. She disappeared, coming up to breathe as her face raised above the water. She let her soft black hair flow around her body as she brought her head below the water level. She looked like the flower my sister was named for, a delicate lily, drifting in the water pool. White shiny skin began to emerge as her body moved in all directions. She stayed briefly, and pulled herself back onto shore, shivering. There were no bulging signs to her body, nothing to indicate she had a baby inside. She quickly assembled her wraps, each layer bringing her more warmth to her shivering body. Looking up at me and waving, she was smiling and laughing like water rolling down the creek. This sound made my hair lay softly around my neck.

With her costume wrapped around her, she finally moved her long hair back and forth, pulling her fingers through it. Then using a quick movement, she wrapped her hair up, placed it around her face and pulled an item from a pocket to secure her hair. What a good feeling to know that bringing her to this creek was going to have a positive effect.

Suddenly, her face became long, replacing the joyful look with determination. She proceeded with a straight back, walking past me back to the cave. I followed. She was walking with purpose again, nothing stopping her. She looked past everything, the birds, even a rabbit eating green plants did not stop her. Mina entered the cave first, with caution. The human was awake, putting on his knapsack. My fear returned, my back-hair stood up, pain followed up my spine. He couldn't leave. He would bring others here!

Mina looked at me, recognizing the danger of his movement. She stood, crossing her hands over her chest, looked directly at the human and said, "You must sit." He wobbled back and forth, disoriented, as his body crumpled to the ground. She was effective! With Mina taking care of him, I started to calm down, the pain was lessening. Why was he here? The word, 'why' was now an important word.

This time, she noisily started to prepare the full tea ceremony, complex in every detail. This noise set up an uncomfortable silence for the human and myself. She was never upset, but this movement told me she was. She roughly threw wood onto the fire, which threw ashes in the air, causing the human to start coughing. His coughing continued, he stood up with no change. The raspy sound continued until she sat him down with water in the bowl.

Finally, with no sign of irritation, she sat down gracefully on her knees, pulling her sleeves up toward her shoulders, and watched until the fire heated the water. She looked at me and at the human, making a gentle, quiet face. She placed the translator on a small flat stone on top of a blue piece of fabric and briefly lowered her head. She started a conversation about how beautiful spring is and its universal meaning on earth. Her hands were busy, adding the tea and pouring the hot water while speaking her words. A light feeling came over me, like sitting in the warmth of the sun. Each movement was slow and graceful. She did not just pick up a cup, but she watched it with full attention as her hands softly moved it through the air. My heart slowed, as if I was still hibernating. I was presented with the largest tea bowl. She gave a small one to the human. We waited until she brought her cup to her lips and drank. I brought my paws around the cup to hold it, but not break it. I thought of it like bird eggs I found, crushed from falling. She passed me some white cake from the small dish. It was a beautiful flower made of colored crystals. I brought it to my mouth when a burst of lemon opened up and down my tongue. I raised my cup and swirled the tea, adding to this fresh feeling inside my body. I thought that this was a dreaming moment, something so pleasurable, that I must be dreaming. We sat, sipping slowly, and she spoke quietly, describing each tea bowl. I realized that this was the first time I was comfortable bringing the bowl to my mouth. Mina changed me. I was learning a lot.

She walked around on her knees, collecting the cups. She focused on each bowl as she held them in her hand. I was surrounded by her magic. It was her small way of doing, repeating movements, bringing warmth to the cave.

Claudius was quiet, but I was reminded that I had not decided what to do with him. If he left, I was in danger of other humans finding us. Humans were my enemy. Suddenly, I was tired of worrying, maybe this was another dream. I was surprised that one minute, I had a calm feeling and then I went right back to hating humans. I looked at Claudius, the human, relaxing as he looked into the fire. Why was he here?

"I must apologize to you." The human spoke as his eyes looked at me. His direct eye contact created waves of anger through my body. My full attention returned to his face, my rising neck fur caused me pain again. I jumped on my back legs, hovering over the human. The human started to shake and I growled at his thin body. I moved to cover the cave entrance with my body. He would not escape. My breath created a sour atmosphere that cloaked the air these humans used. In one swipe, he would die.

Mina grabbed the translator and pushed it in my face. "Speak your words, Pink. Speak your words."

I thought about it. This was not natural for me. I could tear this human apart with just claws. I could throw his body against the wall and he would break apart. Mina continued to repeat, using the translator, "Speak your words."

Could I change my mind about him? He was an enemy, but so slight of build, he was hardly a threat. Okay, I thought, I will speak my words. "I will kill you if you harm Mina." I paused, surprised that she was in my words. Of course, she was. Just like Lily, she was in my heart now. "You cannot leave here; you cannot talk to humans about me." Those words were better. That was my true fear. I felt some relief after speaking.

My stance relaxed as the human showed no signs of aggression, but he did not cower either. He was shaking, still sitting with a straight back.

Suddenly, I realized that I occupied most of the space in the cave with my body. I was pressing their bodies against the wall. I let out my air and made my body smaller. Suddenly, something inside made me wonder. I didn't know humans. I knew that Mina was a human, but she felt different to me. She and I hibernated together and shared stories. She made magic with me. Would this human be different and kill me while I hibernated, my weakest time.

Mina spoke to the human. "You will make a pledge to Pink that you will not ever tell anyone about him. You will not speak about his color, his location nor his habits. Are you willing to give us that promise?"

"Yes, yes, yes," he stuttered. "I promise," as his body slumped down.

"My words to you human are, tell us why you are here. Be quick."

Mina looked concerned and made a hand gesture toward the human. He took a few breaths and looked at both of us. I noticed the leaf-scented air he let out. It was nice.

"I apologize," he repeated again. "I would never harm Mina nor would I talk to humans about your cave, Pink. I would never say anything about this place. I have a reason to be here and I have to tell you why."

His slight body, the gentle way he used his hands, reminded me a little of Mina. I decided to wait, to listen and kill him later, if I needed to.

Mina walked between me and Claudius. "I will help you understand, Pink. What he is going to say is important and I will help. He might be able to help me find Saki!" She was no bigger than a cub, but her strength and courage as she stood at my feet, brought me down off my hind legs. She sat and clearly motioned for me to sit too.

Claudius now spoke in a clear voice, no longer raspy. "I carry a burden of failure. This burden walks next to me everywhere I go. No one likes to be with me. I would never harm anyone because I've already harmed, no, killed, millions of people. No one understands me when I say this. What I did, my actions, affected millions of people. My heart is empty and closed tight. But now, I look at you two in this cave, and I finally see hope. I never thought this would happen. You ask why am I here? I will start by asking you the question." The human turned to Mina. "Did you follow your heart to get here?"

"Did I follow my heart to get here?" repeated Mina. "What do you mean by following my heart?"

"It's simple. I learned from a wise man, one whom you know Mina. He said humans have two choices in life. One is to follow what the brain says. For example, does your brain tell you when to get married and who to marry? Do you marry someone for money with a high status in the village? The second choice is to follow your heart and instead of leaning on security to make your decision, you marry for love. Do you listen to your heart on the way to work? Do you walk the same way to work every day or do you change your route, a small meaningless decision that you make? Do you take the longer path, the scenic route, and do you get to your appointments on time even if your heart yearns to slow down a little? Do you make a meal for your family from the heart or do you make a meal on time? Following your heart is the simple key to the universal law for humanity." He looked at me and added, "The animal kingdom as well, Pink. The animal kingdom does not always live making big decisions, but with many small ones. Instead of thinking with your brain, you can think with your heart, which is following its knowledge, which guides you through a different pathway through life. Heart-love is connecting to the greater good and will create wealth and success, more than any plan conceived by the brain. The brain is over-rated."

"Please stop, Claudius. Did you get this, Pink?"

I thought about his words as they related to Mother. She was always moving, thinking about food and safety. Sometimes when Lily and I played, she would stop and watch us. I thought those times were what this human was talking about. When Mother was worried, we could not feel her heart, but when she watched us, we both sensed her warm feeling toward us. I sensed a difference when she worked on getting food, observing human behavior and preparing for hibernation. "Yes, I follow."

Satisfied, Mina said, "Continue, Claudius."

"Take early invention, like these bowls, for example. Did someone design a bowl, make it to hold tea and use it? No, probably the cook, a woman, would seize rounded stones from the river, honed by centuries of water washing them smooth. She would feel them, admire their rounded purity, and bring them back to her cave. It was the initial attraction woman had to the round, smooth surface that led to the invention of the bowl, I'm sure of it. Not a brainy idea, but one from the heart. In the war between the brain and the heart, the unleashed brain always wins.

So, my simple question is, are you guided by your heart or by your head?"

Mina sat silently erect. There was a long silence. "I know that my heart has guided me here, in the middle of winter, where I almost died. My journey started in the hospital and all I've lived on was my heart energy. My purpose is to find Saki, my lost daughter. In my state, I have nothing else."

"So, you know about this, Mina. For me, not following my heart was my biggest mistake. Even Pink will never cause me the physical harm that matches the pain from my life choices. I would let him eviscerate me and send my misery away, with his strong claws. But now, Mina, I know you understand, but does Pink? We have a small opening to change things."

"Pink will not harm you," interrupted Mina. "Please continue, Claudius. Go slow and I will explain it to him."

"This may be the end of my life with Pink tearing me from limb to limb. But if I have a chance to change history, I will do it, whatever the cost to me."

It was a long while before anyone spoke. I thought about mind and heart. I was learning this and wanted to hear more. The pause was good for me and I think they waited for me to act. I decided to curl down in my corner and show no harm.

"I will now tell you what happened to Klara Pölzl. At the age of 23, Klara was sent to a small town in Upper Austria, Braunau, close to the German border, to be a servant to a large family. I found reasons to travel there and move around the town, pretending to bump into her. She seemed lonely and was always interested in what was happening in Weitra. Once, we had coffee and walked around Palm Park, full of pink wisteria and lilies. The flowers opened her eyes and she leaned down to smell each flower. I remember asking her simple questions like, how are your mother and your sister and your father? I must have bored her to death. I talked about details from my life, traveling in the woods, encountering tall ferns. I shared how I walked 20 miles in one day, so far that I had to take a train to return the same night. At first, I thought she was interested, but it seemed like she was just a polite person and needed company. She never looked into my eyes and she never encouraged me to be physically close to her. Coffees with her burned into my brain, which I replayed over and over in my mind, as I walked. Did I say the right thing to her, was she interested? Walking lessened the burden of my love for her and I wish it hadn't.

"To her, to anyone, I was an immature boy with a crush. When I think about it, I felt something deep inside me. For the first time in my life, I experienced my life path. I knew I was supposed to create life with Klara. I was being directed by one of the most basic of all steam engines, the heart.

"The following year, I was supposed to take a trade and go to Munich for training, which my mother was wildly enthusiastic about. She also suspected that I had feelings for Klara and she was sure it would pass if I pursued this career. I thought it would improve my chances with Klara, so I could be successful enough to support a family and then make Klara my wife. Sadly, when the day came to leave for Munich, I showed more cowardice than usual and refused to get on the train, ran into the woods, and walked all day. I came back that evening, the laughingstock of the town, everyone knew. Someone might have told Klara as well. This incident shamed my parents and left them with no choice but to kick me out of the house. I packed my knapsack, picked a trail, and never looked back. My shame kept me away for years. When I found out that my father died, I returned to take care of my mother who was sick. She was in bed and the frequent visits from the doctor meant that she was staying alive longer than she should. I was shocked at this revelation and wondered why she held onto her life so strongly. She then told me.

"Claudius, I am sad right now. You left us for the wrong reason. I know you were in love and I know that I spent all of my energy making sure you did not find Klara and marry her. I am so sorry. Can you forgive me?"

"I then understood what it means to die with regret, wanting to change those decisions you made early in life. I assured my mother that it was not her fault, but my own. I wanted Klara and all I tried to do was to forget about her."

"It had been five years since I left home. I was slim and muscular in a sinewy way and my face elongated, as with many Austrian men. As I walked through Weitra, I got nice greetings and friendly waves, everyone knowing I was back because of my mother's illness. I also thought people realized that their children did not always follow tradition and have their own ways of living. I noticed more young people from the village took non-traditional paths without parental approval. They may have felt they judged me too harshly. The harsh judgement of my departure was gone. I did not have the heart to ask my mother about Klara as she was too sick, so I just went to Braunau to find out.

"There was not much change in 1890. The bakers, butchers and shoemakers were all there as before and Palm Park looked well maintained. The first thing I found out was Klara married Alois, the proprietor of the house where she was a servant, as his third wife. His previous two wives died. I heard this news from a very gossipy matron, Mrs. Eder, watching children in the park. She also mentioned it was rumored that Klara and Alois were cousins and Klara had a child only four months after they were married. The baby later died of diphtheria. Mrs. Eder said something about men not following Catholic traditions, alluding to Alois' unsavory behavior. She noted, the family did not socialize very much. Klara was now raising a son and a daughter from Alois' previous marriage and only one son of her own, after the deaths of three of her own children. This was a horrible woman, full of humiliating details about Klara and the curse that hung over the household. I was filled with regret of how mistaken I was to walk away from her. That realization stuck in my heart. I should have listened and gone to the end of my desire instead of just walking away from the love of my life in shame.

"Alois was a customs' official, and they lived in a large house outside of town. I found it easily. It was a three-story home, with a steep red-tiled roof and traditional Austrian architecture. Each window was trimmed and painted red with plenty of curly cornices around each window. Mostly residences of this grand design held wealthy people who could afford an architect to design something this special. There were children playing in the yard. The oldest, a boy, was very slim with an odd angular appearance. These must be Klara's children. Why stop here? I asked myself, and knocked on the door. It took a long time for an answer. An older woman, with an apron and a white handkerchief around her neck, asked me in German what I wanted. I asked for Klara and she looked terrified, almost panicky. I peeked inside at the huge buffet in the foyer, the high ceilings and the massive chandelier. I bowed slightly and motioned that I would go, when this old woman grabbed my shoulder. With this strong woman's grasp around my shoulder, I was dragged into the kitchen where I saw Klara. She had her head down, muttering to herself and with two very large cuts on the side of her face. Her hands were red and her head of gold flaxen hair was nodding back and forth with each sob. I paused to think about what I was seeing. She was abused, violently. Was this her husband's doing? I was not sure what to do. I went closer to her to put a hand on her shoulder when she looked up and saw me. The expression of embarrassment and shame was apparent as she motioned for the older woman to show me out.

"After some shouting to the German woman, she slumped over and I stayed, taking a chair next to her. I dressed her wounds with the bandages, neatly stacked on the countertop. I saw other bruises under her dress bodice. This was a nightmare. Everything was surreal. I tried to focus my mind on bandages and iodine. She still looked down. I poured two glasses of brandy. I drank one myself and left her a glass on the counter. I waited, letting her rest and compose herself. The tall son came in the front door and yelled in a high-pitched rage. I've never heard a child yell like that. He stomped his feet, waved his arms, an unusual behavior for any Austrian child. He was yelling that his boots were wet and needed to be changed because his feet were cold. The older woman came over to him and he swung his arm to hit her in the face. I stood up and shouted. I told him to go to his room and he stared at me coldly. Then in a very calm way, he marched up the stairs to the upstairs bedrooms, not looking back and dragging mud all over the carpet.

"All Klara said was, "He's my stepson, Alois, Jr. I cannot control him." She got up, pushing against the chair arm, and walked over to a crib in the kitchen's corner and picked up a baby, maybe one year old. "But this is my son, Adolph." She held him close and pushed his hair back as mothers often do.

"After this shocking scene, I was not sure what to do. It was probably time for me to leave as I could not help and maybe my being here would cause her more damage if her husband found me dressing her wounds. She looked at me in kindness and stared into my eyes. My heart's pain lessened, but the image of her bruised face, "*verbrennen*," scorched my memory. I wondered what it would have been like, had I married Klara. Was she thinking the same thing? As we stared at each other, my big mistake came down hard on me. Why didn't I tell her my feelings when we walked in the park together? All I could do was think of her horrible existence with a violent child and abusive husband. How helpless she was, sitting there in her massive kitchen with everything that anyone could want in life, a husband that provided stability and a small baby to love. And it ended like this. My heart knew she was supposed to be my wife, we were supposed to have lovely children and our future would have been bright. Each day would be filled with the clean, crisp Austrian air and the warmth of sun against the most beautiful backdrop known to man.

"I walked out the front door and back to my mother's deathbed, the image of Klara's cut face and bruised body was on my mind constantly. Could 1 save her, should I save her? As I turned these thoughts in my head, I continued to come back to the real tragedy. I ran away from my heartbreak. As Dr. N. told me, I did not follow my heart. This was a sad realization but the future I struck translated to consequences way beyond my life, her life, and the deaths of millions of people. I did not to listen to my heart. My heart was only a whimper and I lost the most important battle known to civilization in the 20th century.

CHAPTER 9

There was stony silence after Claudius stopped speaking. The fire burned low. Mina was nearest the fire, sitting against a pillow she made by stuffing her Kimono stockings with leaves. Claudius was still sitting like a straight, upright tree sapling. He pulled his slim body onto itself, his overcoat over his shoulders, remaining motionless. I tried to understand everything about his story. I was feeling off center and wanted some quiet from straining to understand. The absence of fear was surprising. I tried to muster some fear because Claudius was a human, but just fell asleep.

I woke to hear Mina speaking to Claudius. "How can you be sure?"

"I've done a lot research. Adolf, the tiny baby I saw in that shocking household, was the tyrannical, monster, Adolph Hitler. I spent hours in the library with Dr. N., researching his family. Only Alois Jr., his step brother and Paula, his younger sister, are still alive. Most everyone talks about how he did not succeed as an artist. I've not read anything about Alois, Jr, the living brother whom I experienced as a bully, nor did I find information on Alois,

Sr. being a physically abusive father, husband and lecher, which I also witnessed. The true answer to Adolph's behavior as an adult has not yet been explained. The two remaining family members Angela and Alois were very discreet and did not speak to anyone about anything related to their family environment. Angela died recently but Alois is still living."

"Dr. N.? Is that Nozomu? The Dr. N. that told you to follow your heart? I met him too."

"I will get to that part of my story, Mina."

"I was wondering about that, your newspaper and the guidance to follow your heart. I'm so interested in why you are here Claudius but please continue with your story. We both experienced WWII resulting in life-changing consequences. Claudius, be realistic. How can you take on the responsibility of the deaths of so many individuals?"

"All I know is if I married Klara, the world would be different. The one man, Adolf Hitler, that decimated the world would not exist. The world would be different but not perfect. So many small incremental changes make up history. There are other tyrannical monsters, like Stalin and Mao, who killed more people than Hitler did."

I noticed Claudius' shoulders lower with his head down and eyes closed.

"I have tried to understand my guilt and rationally argue that I could not know the consequences of my actions and therefore I am not accountable for these lives. But that does not change the fact that millions died from Adolph Hitler's fiendish behavior. A profound truth lies underneath my actions which is I did not follow my heart. I believe this is the core truth of my life. I would like to think if Klara and I had children, we would have a chance at raising children that made a positive difference."

"Claudius, you really cared for Klara and would have dramatically changed her life. I don't think you can put the Holocaust and the deaths of millions of soldiers fighting in WWII on your shoulders. I don't think it is right. However, if what you say is true, and WWII did not happen, then the atom bombs would not have been launched on my hometown and I would be with my family right now, raising my five-year old daughter."

Claudius' face brightened. "Mina, tell the story."

"My journey started August 1945. As I told Pink, I was in Hiroshima when the atomic bomb spread across our lovely city. I was looking at my Japanese maple and feeling very light and happy to have such a lovely garden that literally made my heart sing! So the last event of that day that I remember was looking at the garden and then everything went blank. I woke up at a different time and a different place. My immediate reaction was what about my baby? As far as I could tell, I was alive, but my baby was missing from my body. Nothing was there. No bump, no heartbeat and no information. Everything was gone. I grieved for my baby and initially did not even know where I was. I could understand no one, their white faces looked at me and I just cried and cried. Nothing could console me. I would not eat or drink and was just lost. I was so heavy and full of pain, my heart stopped. There was medical equipment around me, people poking me, sticking needles in me and looking concerned, talking in soft voices that I could not understand.

"For a while, I just stared at the ceiling with tears flowing down my face. Eventually, someone turned on a radio and it was in English. I was interested in figuring out where I was, so I got out of my hospital bed and sat across from a man reading a paper, listening to the radio. He was old, wrinkled and small, looking like a man that lived on our street, wearing a similar hanten jacket. As he looked up from his paper over the rims of his black glasses, he fixated on me. His eyes brightened. He held a blue light in his hands that beamed across the room as he turned it.

He started speaking slowly at first, but like a train going down a hill, he picked up speed and shouted and spoke Japanese so fast, I could not tell what he was saying. His mad appearance attracted a few nurses who tried to restrain him and, finally, someone had a needle which they injected into his arm. They quickly took him away. They brought me back to my room and then left. I could hear the nurses talking quietly but I could not understand them. What was the man saying? He was upset when he spoke. He was trying to tell me something. I needed to cling to an answer, but there was no explanation. Everything around me was western, the food, the clothing, the building, but the strangest was this old Japanese man. I wandered around the hospital, almost invisible, no one paying attention to me. He vanished. I could not ask about him because no one spoke Japanese. For some reason, I believed that he was my key, to understand, and maybe to find my baby.

"I was tired and finally sat down in a visitor lobby and there, directly in front of me, was a newspaper, in English. I could only read the date, 1950. It was five years in the future? What happened? I was consumed with questions and my head pounded. I went back to my bed. I must find that old man. The way he looked at me, I needed to connect with him. I waited until the middle of the night, grabbed my cloth bag holding my kimono, and quietly looked for him, searching each room on my floor. I noticed something strange at the end of the hall with a man sleeping on a chair outside the room. I quietly came to the door which I opened. How can I describe the courage I needed to do this? Courage was a new feeling, but I liked it. That was the beginning of my adventure. This move was what led me on my journey to find Saki. Inside the room was the same old man in bed, wide awake as if he was waiting for me.

"He spoke in a strange Japanese dialect but I understood him."

'There is no time to explain. I am Nozomu-sensei. You have only a small about of time to leave the hospital without causing alarm. Here, take my coat and pants and put your hair under my hat. Now go to the park! I will send help.'

"But I want to know what happened to me. Who are you? Why is the year 1950?" I was panicking.

'No, just take my clothes. It will work out, but leave, leave now and find a bench in the park, across the street!'

"I found his hanten and pants. I left my hospital gown on and tucked it into his pants. There, I was done. He smiled at me and waved me out of the room. As I left the room, I realized that we were speaking in Japanese. The guard at the door was shifting his position, possibly waking up. I turned to the stairway and bolted down four flights. As I found a door at the bottom of the stairs, my heart beat hard, like a Taiko drum. I pushed on the door, throwing my body at it, and found myself outside. The cool air refreshed my burning cheeks. The air was crisp, cool, and smelled like pine needles as the sun was setting. The booming inside my body slowed down."

Mina paused from talking, recognizing I was now awake and listening from the corner. I noticed a lightness in her body, she was sitting very straight and almost hovering above the cave floor. It was like she was waking from a deep sleep. She looked around, her eyes bright, her head turning back and forth, seeing everything for the first time. After Mina stopped her story, I noticed her heart slowed down.

"Oh my," she sighed as she looked at Claudius. "I know about following my heart. My heart has quite a strong voice and can be rather outspoken. My journey, up to now, has not been easy and I find I have to practice patience."

Claudius got up, walked over to Mina, whispering in her ear. The intensity of his eyes was scary and I hoped she was okay with him so close. I shifted my position so Claudius knew I was listening. While their stories were still confusing to me, I wanted to reassure Mina of her safety. I wanted to touch her hand lightly, but I settled for looking directly at her for a long time.

After some time passed, Claudius moved back to his place and she said looking at Claudius, "I understand now." She sat quietly and I welcomed the pause. Mina then looked directly at me and continued her story.

"I had no idea what I was doing, but my heart pounded as I left that hospital. My heart was speaking to me directly. It was just one of the many strange things that I was experiencing. Once I was walking the dark street, my heart said to run away for my life, and do not let anyone catch me. I looked back, but no one was chasing me, and no alarms were set off. Across from the hospital building was a shrine or something like one. The smell of pine trees was strong. I walked on a path that wound around large and small trees, bushes and rows and rows of daffodils. I was surrounded by beauty. This must be the park the old man told me about. What a contrast from the hospital, I thought! As I followed a lighted path, there were benches everywhere. As I slowed down my pace, I realized I had not seen another soul. There were no clues about where I was, but I was more scared that someone was chasing me to take me back so I kept going. As I walked, I enjoyed the blooming azaleas, noting how nicely pruned they were. The richness of the fertile area reminded me of my favorite shrine at home.

"I started getting cold and worried about where I would stay. I was happy to have such a bulky jacket and found a wooden bench, isolated away from the path overlooking a pond, with a brass memorial, in English, containing a name, a message and two dates; 1913-1945. I wondered if this was a memorial bench, was it too sacred to sit on? I sat there anyway, protected by a circle of trees. With my legs pulled inside the jacket, I felt bone-tired. The worst part was my confusion, but I had to push my confusion away as my body said, 'Can I use sleep to give me guidance of what to do next. I was in a different time, place and without any family to help me. I was overcome with sadness which made me sleepy. The jacket provided a pillow, and I lay down, feeling cozy while I smelled sweet tobacco coming from one of the many pockets.

"Sleep did not come. My first thought was about my unborn child. Where was she and what happened to her? Suddenly, I was crying and my heart now cramped up, beating slowly. This deliberate, dark beat took over my whole body. It would have been a horrible moment, but instead, I started to feel happy as I shifted to the memory of feeling of my baby inside of me. Actually, I thought she was someplace close. A strong idea came to me. She was someplace strange and different, just as I was. Maybe some other woman was carrying her. I suddenly realized my purpose. I must find my baby. Yes, that was what I had to do. Once that thought became clear, my body relaxed and the heaviness was lifted. I felt calm."

Mina paused, straightened her back and looked at Claudius. "Claudius. I went from Hiroshima, 1945, to Durham, North Carolina, 1950. I traveled in time and location. Dr. Nozomu calls this Time Travel."

"Was that Dr. Nozomu in the hospital?"

I added, "Time travel? Speak slowly, Mina. What is time travel?" My mind was just catching up to my speech. I desperately wanted to understand. There was something happening and my whole body was involved. Involved in listening deeply, as if there was an answer for me. Something that would change, but I did not know what that was.

Mina smiled and took a long breath in and let it out, extending a sweet lemony smell around the cave. "I think it will help if I finish my story first and then we can talk about travel and Dr. Nozomu." She stretched her arms up in the air, like a butterfly opening up to fly for the first time. Her robes moved as air filled the wings and they fell back as she adjusted her sitting position and continued. "I was laying on this bench and wondered, where was my husband? Our parents? I did not feel any different. My questions did not impact me like they should. I was more afraid of the hospital looking for me than how I ended up in 1950, in an English-speaking country. Was I in the US? We were at war with the US, but this was five years in the future. What happened to the war? And how did I get here? My thoughts circled with no ending. They kept bringing me back to my garden and the baby I was carrying until I finally fell asleep on the bench. My last thoughts were of the white light that changed everything.

"Of course, since then, I've researched everything. My position was five hundred feet from ground zero. On Monday, August 6, 1945, at 8:15 AM, the Atomic Bomb "Little Boy" dropped on Hiroshima by an American B-29 bomber, the Enola Gay, directly killing an estimated 80,000 people. By the end of the year, injury and radiation brought total casualties to 90,000 to 140,000. Approximately 69 percent of the city's buildings were completely destroyed, and another 7 percent severely damaged. No one survived where I stood. Only through this special time-travel did I endure."

Claudius stood up to stoke the fire. "Mina, I know about the Hiroshima bomb. It seems impossible that you survived. If you were near the center, where the bomb landed, you would not survive. This single act ended World War II."

"Yes, Claudius, I know how strange this sounds but let me continue. As I woke from the bench, stretching, pushing my legs onto the ground, I heard birds. The strong smell of gardenia, warmed by the sun, came from a plant right behind me. I left the jacket on the bench and looked around. It was a beautiful day, and I felt renewed, as if I slept on a futon at home. Two small pale white dogs, very cute, came up to me and played with my baggy pants. Before I knew it, I was leaning down, petting their soft, curly white hair. A young girl ran toward me. She looked like my younger sister, very pale, long braided dark hair, black pants, white short-sleeved shirt. She had a tattoo with lines of a long, black and blue-green tattoo curling up her left arm. It looked like a snake, wrapping around a Lotus flower starting at her wrist. Such a young girl with a tattoo! She was out of breath, having chased the dogs, and said, '*Konichi-wa, Sumimasen.*' I was shocked to hear a greeting in my language.

We played with the dogs for a while and then sat on the bench together. She was as beautiful as the gardenia flowers that blossomed around us. I introduced myself in Japanese and said that my place of origin was Japan, specifically Hiroshima. I added I was looking for my child. The words spilled out quickly and the young girl looked at me kindly, without concern. She looked around at the bench until she saw the blue jacket. She stared at it for a long time. 'This reminds me of a friend's hanten, jacket.'

"It is very hard to describe these moments of confusion, then relief. One moment, I was happy, playing with these dogs and exchanging a few words in Japanese, and the next moment, I could scream and wish I had answers. Her dogs loved me. After playing a while, I fell to the ground, sobbing. The girl immediately helped me back onto the bench and said, in Japanese, she wanted to bring me to her home.

"I tried to say no, but could only shake my head. At that point, I realized I needed to compose myself and make sure I did the right thing. I needed to get away from the hospital in case they were looking for me. I collected my thoughts, checking in before speaking and then these words poured out of me. 'I need help. I do not know where I am, I only speak Japanese, I do not have clothes or food or shelter. I am not sick. No hospital, please!' As the sun rose, I felt it on my face, warming my skin. The coolness of the night was replaced with a warm sunny hug.

"I remember taking two long breaths, needing to exhibit control. I was thinking about my education. I did not speak any language other than Japanese, I could make beautiful letters of Kanji characters, I could tune a lute and make delicate *ikebana,* using well-chosen pottery. While this education brought me and my husband together in marriage, I could not use it now. I tried to recall the maps I studied in school, but my memory was vague. I never traveled outside Japan and the rest of the world was full of foreigners, *gaijin*. I knew what English sounded like from the missionaries at the Christian church and knew that was the language that was being spoken in the hospital. I suddenly felt a wave of overwhelm and loneliness. What should I do next?

'Oh, my.' She patted my hand and said, "I can help. Don't worry, we're not going back to the hospital. My name is Kiko. I live with my parents and I was born here, but they were born in Japan. My parents are both scientists and they are studying the effects of atomic radiation in people who survived the Atomic Bomb in both Hiroshima and Nagasaki. They work at Duke University. I will take you home to meet them. They are going to help you. You can follow me and Toto and Terro, my dogs, back to our home." She was friendly, but firm with her offer. Her strength gave me no choice but to accept her plan. The dogs' playfulness helped stabilize my opinion of the situation.

"I nodded and picked up the jacket and cloth bag containing my kimono. We walked the path, following Toto and Terro with Kiko chatting in English, in a very soft voice. Kiko pointed to several spots in the garden as the warm sun and flowers relaxed me. I already accepted she was going to take me to a safe place and even help me.

"Switching to Japanese, she apologized for speaking English. Japanese was her second language and she was not accustomed to speaking only Japanese for long time periods. She then talked at length about tamamono bushes and how she hated that they were pruned into a tight ball. I agreed with her. The ones in this garden were shaped gracefully and naturally. The azaleas were still in bloom; pink and beautifully arranged. The pond mirrored a beautiful reflection of tall white pines, framing the whole picture. As we walked around the park, I was feeling strong."

Mina's whole body, face and hands were a picture of serenity as she spoke. Each description of the park helped me understand what made her happy.

"Once we left the park, my eyes opened wide as a different world opened up. The road was wide and busy with dark black cars and open trucks moving in three directions. Cars were dominant here and people walking, like us, were vulnerable. Nevertheless, we navigated the busy street as I stayed close to Kiko and her dogs. After crossing, we entered a quiet street with houses built close to each other, with concrete walks on both sides. They looked like the cottages I saw in picture books about America. It was then when I fully realized one impossible thing, I was in America. The houses, the green lawns and the cars were all American! The people were dressed in western clothes, men with ties and women in dresses with bows, high heels and stockings. Most people ignored us, but a few looked at me with surprise, in my oversized pants and coat. I felt sad, leaving the park behind. This world made me feel alone, strange and homesick.

"We came up to a gray house, one story, with a low slanted roof. The house was smaller and lower to the ground than most of the houses on the block. Kiko motioned for me to enter the house, and we both stooped to take off our shoes at the same time. The dogs ran in, excited to be home, and raced back and forth in the front room. Suddenly, I felt safe. There was a tatami room to my left with a low table, cushions and a beautiful *butsudan* against the wall. There was a small kitchen next to it and, in the back of the house, a long panel of *washi* that opened out onto a garden pond with *koi*! Then, I could not believe what I was seeing. In the very back of the garden was a Japanese maple, very similar to the one I was looking at when the light changed my life.

'I'll make tea and some food for us to eat. You must be hungry.'

"She told me to sit and enjoy the garden while she boiled water and heated miso soup for breakfast. Good smells came from the kitchen and I was so surprised how my stomach growled out loud. I was hungry. Kiko brought out a tray with many lovely foods, arranged perfectly and that strangely even matched the tea fragrance. I still could not believe my luck. I always heard that western food was different and not very good. I had nothing to worry about. This food was a traditional Japanese breakfast with miso soup, smoked trout, eggs and lovely seaweed, spiced perfectly. We sat down and slowly selected parts from each dish with chopsticks. Kiko loved smoked trout and finished each morsel of the fish. Her bones were arranged back again, as if the fish was still intact. I was intrigued by her display of this kind of talent. We ate and looked out at the garden. Again, I was happy and comfortable. I must be in the right place, I thought.

"The dogs came into the room, not looking for food, but sat and settled into this beautiful scene of serenity and peace. My journey brought me here, far from Hiroshima, but I was struck that I could not logically figure out how I got here. We were at war with the rest of the world and there was no way to take a boat or a plane to America. What was even stranger is I was getting used to this new body with the sad realization I lost my baby. No setting, even one this beautiful, could remove the grief I was feeling."

The cave was getting dark. Claudius got up and stoked the fire, creating a small blaze. Mina's story about a nice breakfast was making me hungry, so I thought about what we could eat. I left the cave as Claudius ran to join me. I ignored him as we walked around the outside of the cave in a spiral fashion. I found a large cache of pecans that I foraged last fall, protected underneath a rock against a limestone cliff. Spring is not an abundant time in the woods. Anything that lived through the snowy winter was of poor nutrition. I dug up soft wild yams, hickory nuts and grabbed the few dried blackberries still on the trees. Claudius helped as we brought everything we gathered back to the cave. Mina took charge immediately. She roasted the nuts, ground them into flour, added water from the tea pot and created small disks she called bread. She also took a few nuts and tossed them around with some greens she collected that were growing outside the cave, under the snow. Claudius placed the roots around the coals to bake. He was very excited about eating them. He called them *Yamswurzel*.

As we ate, I thought about Mina's story and when she talked about her baby and how sad she felt, the same way I felt about Mother and Lily. What was different now was my mind was busy listening and I wanted to use the translator and say something about my agony of loss. I felt a physical ache which I could relieve if I stood up and moved. I grabbed the translator.

"I also was in great pain for a long time. After my sister left, I had a lot of time to be by myself. Everything needed me to act. All of the things we shared were gone. I needed to think about each step, what to do and how to do it. Everything was hard. I struggled, answered my complaints, resisted and continued to go in circles. I stayed that way for a long time. My heart was quiet and my mind just took over. The pain of losing my mother and now my sister was buried someplace in my body. The pain moved around, sometimes in my neck, sometimes as a bellyache and sometimes through my eyes, as my world dimmed. I was more reckless and on the verge of losing the protection of deep woods. This was a terrible time for me and I had to change.

"One day, I sat by the creek, watching the water flow downstream. Water flows in a pattern, but also changes constantly. Minnows, fish, crawdads moved as I observed without any interest in catching them for food. The algae reflected light in different ways, the arrangement of rocks alongside the river banks and their size and position as the creek twisted and turned, all seemed significant. As the day passed, my focus on stream activities remained, as I felt sorrow leave my body. With a fully awake mind, I was peaceful. Many of the irritating pains in my body disappeared. My heart was not seizing up as the heart muscles relaxed. I was totally relaxed and contented."

Claudius turned toward me directly. "There must be something about this place as I just had a similar experience. I sat and filled my head with the vision of falling in air, but never reaching ground. It was like feeling air passing by me as I glided down. I was not floating, but swimming in place through the air. I felt like you did, Pink, relaxed, contented, very aware of everything around me. What a gift this place is, Pink."

For some reason, I did not feel uncomfortable with his attention. What he said gave me joy, another word I learned about. I had a feeling of joy that he understood something about me and we were connected, knowing that we felt the same thing, together.

"Let me continue my story to explain why I am here. I also want to know why you are here, Claudius." Again, she shifted her position, readying us to pay attention to her. "As you recall, I followed this young girl, Kiko, to her home. She and I had a lovely afternoon, taking tea and viewing their beautiful Japanese garden off the living room. That is where we were sitting when Kiko's parents came home. If I surprised them with my presence, they did not show it. They said they were preparing dinner and Yoko, Kiko's mother, went into the kitchen, closed the shutters to the kitchen, which left Kiko's father, Nobu, to sit and converse with us. He wore round, black-framed glasses and a simple white shirt and thin necktie with black pants. He kneeled on the floor, and his eyes looked out, as if he was seeing the Japanese garden for the first time. He talked about how difficult it was to find the right stones for this garden in America and how he and his friends went to the Appalachian Mountains, searching for each stone individually. He hired two men to put them in place, two-thirds of each stone buried below the soil level. His design for the garden was organized around the placement of the three stones. He said that it was a chance encounter with a Japanese friend that he was able to add koi to the garden, a recent addition. He showed no pride in his accomplishment, but maintained a quiet manner, simply stating what he did. Meanwhile, Yoko was making the noise of cooking with smells of home seeping through the shutters. Everything felt natural, like home to me and I was no longer homesick.

'I turned to look at Nobu and found him staring at me. I immediately apologized for my appearance and explained to him how I woke up in the hospital, not knowing how I got here. I explained my escape and spending the night in the park in this old man's hanten jacket, that kept me warm. I told him Kiko was wonderful and how grateful I was to have someone help out and introduce me to this world.

"I shared the last memory of my garden, how the image of the bright light has stayed with me. Waking up in a hospital bed was my next memory without my baby. I was in a new body, still alive. It made no difference to me because I believed Saki was still living. She was named Hope. I had no choice but to find her."

CHAPTER 10

"As I spoke about this experience, I realized that the noise in the kitchen stopped and there was absolute silence. Nobu looked at me with the kindest eyes. He bowed deeply and lifted his head to look at me closely. He then got up to help Yoko prepare the food. It was apparent that Nobu and Yoko were communicating softly, but fervently during this time.

"It was strange, how much I accepted this situation without question. I enjoyed the serene moments the garden brought me. Kiko also turned quiet, with her dogs sleeping on both sides of her. We moved to the beautiful tatami room, complete with a low lacquer table, as Yoko presented many dishes individually. She pulled up the sleeve of her white blouse, showing a similar tattoo as Kiko's, only darker with the deep colors of blue and green. She caught me staring at it and smiled.

'My mother's tradition," said Yoko. 'We belong to a mother-line, which Kiko was initiated into when she was sixteen. This tattoo will last her whole life and save her from unwanted spirits.

We asked her if she wanted it over and over, and she always insisted.'

Nobu said that when they moved to the United States, they tried to keep as many traditions as they were able. They traveled by steamer, bringing their tatami mats, this table and several furniture pieces. They were forever grateful as they had no plans to return for many years. I noticed that the tea cups were exquisite. The artist's name on the cups was someone I knew. What a coincidence, this artist lived only one hundred feet from my house. We continued to talk about Japan, each speaking about what they missed and what they loved about living in the United States. They had an active research community in Raleigh and enjoyed getting together with people from China, Korea, Germany, the United Kingdom and Americans. After dinner, we moved back to the living room and Nobu changed his expression, deep creases framed his face.

'I have a lot of things to share with you that may open some windows,' said Nobu. 'I have to warn you that this information will create even more uncertainty for you. We will support you as much as we can. We, Yoko and I, and a group of scientists are doing research on the effect of radiation on human beings. Early on, this research was not funded, but we are finally seeing some interest for our efforts by the United States and Japan. Keloids are a consequence of nuclear exposure. We are also tracking genetic changes of future generations. We are creating a large file of information to follow as many people as we can and medically confirm the consequences of this bomb for future generations. We have a good idea of what radiation sickness is like and the probability of the radiation sickness as a factor of the distance of what we are calling ground zero, the epi-center of the bomb. My wife and I have a wall-sized map of Hiroshima City in our laboratory that supports our studies. From our understanding of the location of your house, it is 100% impossible for you to be a survivor of such a blast. No one survived in this area and the nearest casualties were 5 miles from the epicenter of the bomb and those individuals survived depending on literally where their heads were turned.' He paused a moment and then said, 'This bomb had devasting effects against mankind. The debate regarding if this was the correct choice to end the war will never go away.

'Mina, I cannot say much right now, but tomorrow morning, if you agree, we will take a drive to a remote place in South Carolina. When I say remote, I mean no electricity and it is located deep in the forest of the Smoky Mountains. I will introduce you to an individual who will provide answers for you. You will not be harmed and I think you will be taking a step in the right direction.'

"Kiko sat closer to me and she picked up my hand to hold it. Toto and Terro came over too. Koko and Nobu were making up a bed for me while I sat sandwiched between two dogs.

"All right, this is where everything became wildly mysterious for me. That night, I slept in a tatami room with an extra-long futon and big quilt, I felt so small. I lay there, trying to sort everything out in my mind, but instantly fell asleep. This was so much better than a bench in the park. Everyone got up early and enjoyed a wonderful warm breakfast prepared by Yoko. It was a cool morning. Kiko lent me a long dress and I wore the hanten, and carried my kimono bag. It was a Saturday. The roads were absent of people and cars. Nobu was informing me of many things about modern life in America. I listened and looked out the window of the car at everything from the back seat. The city roads became dirt roads, which I enjoyed immensely. I saw tall pine trees and even a bamboo grove. We passed thought many towns, small clusters of houses with big front porches wrapping around each house. People walked at a slower pace than the city and often stared at this big black car. I sat in the back seat next to Kiko, I was happy to not have to communicate very much. Nobu stopped talking to me about America and I just enjoyed the different shades of green and bright bursts of color from the bushes and trees.

"After passing through a city called Charlotte, we added fuel to the car. We all stretched and sat down in a diner to have lunch. I was surprised at everything about that place. Everything was more foreign than the city of Durham. We traveled until almost dark when the car slowed down finally and turned into a smaller road. The road went directly into deep woods with lots of uneven ruts. The car rolled, throwing us on top of each other. This went on for a while until we came to a clearing where there was a long modular sandstone building with flowers at each entrance. We stopped and got out. As I walked amongst the beauty of tall pines, magnolia trees in full bloom, and rows of azaleas, my head was free of worries. A door opened and people surrounded us. They were talking amongst themselves and spoke many different languages, including Korean, Mandarin, German and English. They were so enthusiastic in their welcome, opening their arms, making eye contact and gesturing widely as if we were royalty. We were so physically close, I needed to move away to breathe. They laughed and Nobu bowed several times. We were told to drive further down the road.

We came to a compact house called a cabin with two rooms. We left our bags there and then piled back into the car and drove a little further. We came to a large clearing surrounding a circular building built with field stone. It was beautiful with a view of mountains behind it. This time, no one came out to greet us. Nobu got out and arranged the creases on his pants. Yoko brushed Nobu's shoulders, cleaned his glasses for him and handed them back. I was not comfortable with grand gestures, so I just stood quietly, waiting to see what the fuss was about. We approached the door as a group, knocked and entered, no one greeting us at the door. The outer wall was circular, filled with neatly stacked books, journals and papers, floor to ceiling. As we walked to the right, the stacks looming over our heads, we came to an opening on the left. I was the last to enter and Nobu's family lined up behind a circle of alternating chairs and cushions. A small Shinto shrine was set in the middle of the circle with a man sitting on a cushion opposite us, deep in concentration. Suddenly, he got up, walked toward Nobu and extended a bright smile. He then welcomed each of us, bowing and extending gestures to sit down. I looked at him as he approached me last and realized he was the same man I saw in the hospital. He smiled knowingly with a familiar greeting. '*Dozo yoroshiku onegaishimasu.*'

'*Hajimemashite,*' I responded, nice to meet you.

"Dr. Nozomu and you have met, yes?" asked Nobu.

"Yes, we met in the hospital. This is his coat," I said as I thanked him and handed it back. Dr. Nozomu took the coat and motioned for me to sit down next to him. His subtle gesture toward me settled my nerves. I had so many questions about the hospital, the year, this location. He must have answers. I willed patience, even though my mind had so many questions. Tea was being prepared and cups were passed around. The last cup on the tray was mine. It had blue and white colors that extended around the edge like clouds on a bright sunny day, with a small red smudge on the opposite side. I smiled and commented, "I'm wondering about the meaning of my cup."

"Dr. Nozomu did not look happy with my question as his flat smile turned down slightly. Finally, he answered me, 'Only you will know the significance.' So not to ruin the moment, I tried to enjoy the bright flavor of the tea, while my mind raced. What did that mean? Sitting in this circle was a perfect counterbalance to the craziness of the past two days. Feeling a sense of peace with so many people I did not know was unique. The lingering smell of burning sage hung over the group, and someone said it cleared the way of negative thoughts. I was now hopeful my big question, what happened to my baby, would be answered.

"Dr. Nozomu looked at me as he examined his coat. He said he was grateful I brought his coat back. He only mentioned the coat, nothing else. "Then Dr. Nozomu revealed how he escaped the hospital. I concentrated as he slowly shared his story; this had a calming effect on me. While he was in the hospital, he needed to escape. Just like me. Once they discovered I was missing, people ran around, looking for me. During this chaos, he put on a lab coat and walked out. He thanked me for the diversion."

I made a sound from my throat, I was excited about her story. Claudius sat taller, more erect. Mina seemed unsure until she looked into my eyes. "Please continue, Mina." Claudius nodded in agreement.

"I was sure Nobu and Yoko were part of what was feeling like a grand scheme. They showed no surprise as he talked about his escape, but I did not need any distractions from my question. I asked the doctor, 'What's going on? I was at the epicenter of Hiroshima and ended up in the hospital.' As my anxiety rose, Dr. Nozomu's calm face helped me relax. He said our stories needed to be told first. This might not have made any sense to me but the tone he set reduced my anxiety as my curiosity piqued.

"Dr. Nozomu began by picking up his jacket and looking inside. He pulled a vertical zipper, placed his hand inside and pulled out a round blue object. He handed it to me and as I turned it in my hands, it glowed a beautiful blue color, shifting to violet and then green. It vibrated in my hand and felt warm. This beautiful blue globe, Dr. Nozomu called it an Orb, transferred energy from my hand onto my arm. Dr. Nozomu told me to put it in the center of the circle where there was a small platform. I hated to release it, but as we sat and watched, it glowed and vibrated. Everyone was mesmerized.

"Shall we take a break? My story is long."

Claudius and I shook our heads no and Claudius said, "Continue please!"

"Dr. Nozomu said this Orb was critically important to finding answers. He said he was part of a group responsible for its invention and promised that the unusual circumstances that brought us together would eventually become clear. The group in the circle faded from my awareness and I felt a bright light pass through me.

'Let's try something, Mina.' He breathed deeply in through his nose, then followed with an outbreath that was very loud. He placed his knuckles below his chin and continued to breathe in and out in this noisy fashion. The noise was addictive as I breathed with him. Now the group was breathing together. The Orb in the center glowed from bright blue to dark blue, deepening the color intensity as the vibrations intensified. Each time the group took a breath, pulling in more air and then pressing out with their lungs, the Orb's glow expanded, covering the circle in a vibrant violet color. I felt like I could touch it with my hand, but my body was still shaking with each inhale. The device lifted from its spot in the center of the circle, the violet color now reaching above our circle as the breathing continued. This seemed like it was normal, but I could not stop shaking. Finally, Dr. Nozomu slowed his breathing, and then each person slowed in a unified rhythm. The Orb descended back to the platform and returned to its original bright blue color. Everyone relaxed, sighed, shifted their position. I was exhausted and melted into my cushion. Everyone commented on the Orb, sharing their experiences, but no one seemed to be surprised that the Orb rose against gravity. I wanted to know more about it. I wanted to understand why I had the Orb in the pocket of Dr. N's Hanten. Strange things were happening. I looked at Kiko and Nobu and they were quiet, not shaking like I was.

"Once the talking stopped, Dr. Nozomu said to me, 'Mina, you are close to finding something out, this is why you are shaking.

I suggest that we leave you alone with the Orb so you can practice working with it. Please repeat the breathing exercise we just did and we'll come back a little later. This is a serious instrument, but it will bring you hope and confidence in finding answers. It is important that you feel comfortable and balanced. Breathing will help you with this. Focus only on those things that will clear your mind and open your heart. I know this sounds strange, but you will know exactly what I mean, once you get started.' Everyone stood up. They looked kindly toward me, using their hands as gestures and some even bowed. But I was scared. They left the room quickly and Dr. Nozomu stayed with me silently for a while and then left me alone. I was in full panic mode. Being alone was strange and now there was some expectation for me to practice with this Orb. What if I could not do this? My mind took over for a while until I noticed the short breaths I was taking. My mind continued to wrap me in self-defeat. This was not going well.

"As I sat with the glowing object, my heart beat fast and my breath sharp, I thought I would just get up and leave the room. What was I supposed to do? I needed more information. They abandoned me, leaving me to fail. While I was ruminating, the object glowed red and beat fast in an irregular disturbing way. Suddenly, I felt responsible for the Orb. The red color started pulsing against my heart's natural rhythm. The disruptive cadence was affecting me and I felt like I was back in Hiroshima, feeling my baby and dying from the red heat. Everything was falling apart. The beating was louder and louder. I wanted to turn it off but surrendered to my fate. This Orb was not the answer and was going to kill me of a heart attack or asphyxiation. The beating went away momentarily. I tried taking a breath, I needed oxygen to live. My heart seized up for a moment and I tried to breathe in. I tried to pull in air, I noticed the Orb was showing a dark red color, a red purple, followed by a blue purple, violet. I continued with deeper and deeper breaths, no longer gasping. The glowing ball turned from deeper violet to indigo, and finally the vibration slowed to a natural rhythm, that matched my normal breathing rhythm. When I found that I could control my breath and that changed the Orb, I felt a wave of calm from my toes to my head. As I breathed deeper, my mind quieted down, no longer filled with fear for my baby's life. As my heart replaced my thoughts, I suddenly felt my baby, her presence in my body. This tiny human, Saki, Hope. I spoke to her with a soft tone, out loud. I told her not to worry, that I would help her, that I was going to protect her. I filled my heart with the awareness of her and the Orb turned a sapphire-blue that lit the ceiling of the room with soft blue light. The room was filled with love. My heart now felt open, raw and vulnerable. As I sat there, I felt love inside my heart, as I remembered sitting in my garden in Hiroshima.

"I'm not sure I can continue." Mina took a breath, her eyes now focused on the cave door, staring. Light was reflecting from the few remaining ice crystals, spreading all colors of the rainbow onto the cave wall. "There." She paused and smiled. "This rainbow is a sign. I think I can do this. I can finish the story." Her voice was softer as she adjusted her sitting position, crossed both hands on her heart and continued.

"When I woke up, the room was the same, the Orb looked like the blue ceramic ball that came from the hanten jacket, and I was still alone. I remembered everything and started to connect the feeling of my baby's presence with the Orb. I sat as a wonderful glow covered my body and, momentarily, I felt my baby's energy swell inside of me and then disappear. It was strange how I manifested her energy using the Orb. I was not sure what I was doing, but if I rested and tried again, I thought I could repeat it.

"Slowly, the people came back to the circle. Nobu, Yoko and Kiko surrounded me with attention and soft, kind words. Dr. Nozomu came into the room last and everyone eased into their seats. Energy moved up my spine, and I smiled to myself. I felt clear of confusion and relished that rare moment."

Mina's appearance changed. The fire burned low, so I got up and stoked it. It was like she was waking up, looking around. Reliving the time with Dr. Nozomu, Kiko, Nobu and Yoko gave her extra energy.

"I think I can continue. I remember the sweet smell of wisteria of that place. I can even pick up the sound of a burning candle and each detail of the room. I need to keep going. Telling the story is giving me a second insight. Now where was I?

"Once the room became quiet, Dr. Nozomu looked at everyone in the eye."

'We will now share a meal and convene tomorrow morning at 9:00 AM.' Everyone rose from their chairs and cushions, talking and moved into another room to a huge spread of food. The whole experience was straining my patience and I just wanted to sleep. As the group moved into the dining room, I realized I was hungry. I don't remember much except, Kiko and I left early while the adults talked late into the evening.

The next morning, the circle convened on time. We conducted the breathing exercise using the Orb's response in colors of the rainbow and ending in sapphire-blue. Dr. Nozomu then explained that we were in an honorable circle of which each participant had equal responsibility. Each person would add their true self, their truth, into the center of the circle. He said if everyone spoke authentically, the circle would be whole and each piece represented. He also said to us that no one could speak about or repeat what was said in the circle. As random as life itself, each individual told a story about themselves, talking about difficult times, adding nuances of detail, bringing each story to life. I was surprised. The stories were so personal, so private.

"After each person spoke, there was a pause, and often, someone would sigh loudly. I was curious about this. The group seemed to take in what was said, not asking questions, just as the doctor requested. As each person shared, the words manifested slowly into an image inside the circle that eventually disappeared into the air after they finished. I imagined each time someone sighed, it was about loss. His or her words would be treasured as just that moment. It was interesting that even the blue Orb would change color and brighten, or dim, in response to what was spoken. The group created collectively a supernatural, numinous experience. It took the entire morning and I never got tired or lost energy. This sharing provided me with insights into my life experiences and I never lost concentration.

"Finally, Dr. Nozomu spoke. He looked at me. 'I am burdened with many things that I need to do. But only when everything is resolved, can I continue my work. I need to make peace with my past and follow my heart. I cannot afford to make a mistake now and I must respect myself and not walk away from this challenge.'

"I listened, wondering what Dr. Nozomu was talking about. I hoped I was not the burden he referred to. He continued with a story from his youth and his challenges of going his own way versus the way his parents wished he would go. The image he manifested inside the circle looked like the blue ocean with a bright orange sunset that slowly set as his story came to an end. The story made me sad."

"Dr. Nozomu told me it was my time to share. I remembered the meaning of his name in Japanese, Nozomu meant, 'Hope.' The ball vibrated a blue color balanced with green and the color of teal. I was quiet as I looked into the ball, I felt myself going inside my body with my mind as the calmness spread from head to toe. I was not nervous about speaking, but words were stuck in my throat. I choked up. Then a grief took over, so strong that tears streamed down my face. I felt detached and did not expect this. When I looked up, eleven loving faces were looking at me. My breath filled my lungs, and the air flowed out, my body shuddering, now big tears moved down my face. My body was shaking. I looked down and waited; still no words came to me. My mind shut down completely. Typically, I would panic if this happened, but I just waited, controlling my breath as it slowed down. Suddenly, my own words rolled out of my mouth."

"I was then able to speak about what happened to me before this circle of strangers. Let me correct that statement; they were not strangers anymore. I could now get words out and explain. Sharing where I came from, how my baby was in me at the time of the bomb, how I woke up in a different body, five years later on the other side of the world. I felt full, loving attention from the group. No one broke concentration. It was so supportive. I could talk about my garden and how happy I was in minute detail, feeling the words reaching across the circle, and land on understanding hearts.

"Finally, I was complete. Curious about my feeling of both exhaustion and emptiness. I asked Dr. Nozomu what to do.

"He sat for a while as I waited for his answer. Everyone in the circle closed in, in order to hear his words. 'Of course,' he said, 'follow your heart. Use your heart to answer big questions. Always keep moving. Take each step as if it is the correct one. Jump into the abyss, knowingly.' He looked at everyone in the tightly closed circle and said, "This advice is for everyone. Lingering too long on a problem creates a fresh set of challenges, barriers to your dreams." Then he turned toward me, his full attention. "Mina, this Orb is for you. Power from the Orb will be a challenge for you so use it carefully. Trust yourself."

"The circle broke up. This experience was powerful and I was surprised as each person approached me with kind words and gestures. I must have repeated my gratitude many times. *Sumimasen, Sumimasen.* I realized that everything was okay as the group showered me in kindness and soothing gestures. They were also opening their hearts, and no one experienced anything but love. Finally, we all got up and joined hands. After that, each person walked around, holding, hugging and talking to each other. It was strange to realize that I was part of the group, woven together with these personal stories. Gradually, each individual slowly left the building until just Kiko, Nobu, Yoko and I were left standing with Dr. Nozomu.

"I no longer had questions. I was certain of my direction. Dr. Nozomu gave me the jacket and placed the now plain ceramic ball inside the pocket of the hanten.

"Mina," he said solemnly, "this belongs to you for now.

'Dr. Nozomu,' I asked, 'can I use it to find my baby?'

'The Orb identified you and it will play a major role in your quest to find Saki.

"Saying her name, Saki, refreshed my thoughts. Her name was Saki, female for hope. "How do you know her name?' I asked.

"I know a lot about Saki. She is hope for me as well."

"What should I do now?"

"Go back with Yoko and Nobu. Spend time acquainting yourself with society. Then when you are ready come back and we will get started working with the Orb." He said with a soft, loving smile.

"I was confused and relieved. Both emotions battling for my attention. I thanked him and said I would wear his hanten with pride and respect.

"We got into the car again and worked our way back onto the dirt road. Rain was pouring, the sound beating hard onto the hood. Nobu was leaning forward, having trouble seeing the road and water was rising in low spots. I sat in the back seat again, practiced my breathing and tried to remove bad thoughts about the rain, the road and my Saki. I woke up at midnight just as we reached home. We entered the house and the same bed was prepared for me. I carefully took off the jacket, noticed the Orb looked like a dull ceramic object. I left it in the coat, secure. I needed to rest, from it, from everything."

Mina stood up, in a trance, as if she was still inside her story. "I'm tired now. Tomorrow, I will continue." She went to the carved-out hole she was now used to sleeping in and laid her head down on her jacket.

CHAPTER 11

It was difficult to stay quiet while Mina slept. Her story was still in my head. I got up to leave and shake it off. Claudius also stood up and reached for the translator. It dropped onto Mina's robes and he reached down to pick it up, moving the folds of cloth. I left him behind as it was sunny and birds were singing. The air was still cool and green plants were emerging from under clumps of snow, mixed with brown debris left over from fall.

I noticed he did not follow me, but walked directly toward the lake. I followed. He stopped, turned to me and lifted the translator with his hand. "Pink, we have come a long way together. I am beginning to feel safe around you. It's important that you trust me. We have a lot to do to prepare."

I said, "Prepare?"

"Yes, prepare is a word that you would use in the fall. You prepare for hibernation. You do things that help you survive in winter, right?"

I sat. Yes, prepare, was a word I now understood about the fall. Why is Claudius preparing for hibernation?

"Pink, do you remember when Mina held the Orb? You watched her. How did she hold the Orb and what did you see?"

"I will show you where she stood." We walked up to the three stones that reached out toward the deepest part of the lake. "She was sitting on the largest of the three stones, over there."

He stood for a long time, looking at the stones, dropped the translator and then walked out to the largest stone. His movements were slow, carefully placing both feet on each stone before going on to the next. Once he reached the last stone, something changed. He raised his arms to the sky, he moved with his body, making slow movements. It reminded me of Mina's movements, only slow. He walked back, grabbed the translator and found a place to lean against the closest tree. He was tired again.

I left him and found Mina coming out of the cave. "Where is Claudius?" she asked. The space between her eyes was no longer smooth. Words came out of her mouth quickly, but even without the translator, I knew she was upset. I showed her to the location where Claudius slept. Words too fast to understand were spat onto Claudius from her mouth. Mina was agitated!

He flailed back to her like a fly stuck in a web. He was a small, weak human, not dangerous. He started a rhythmic breathing cycle and looked brittle, like dry wood. Once he quieted down, he spoke to Mina. "It's important for me to finish my story, Mina. You will understand when I share more information."

"No, I don't care about your story. Where is the Orb?" she shouted.

Claudius' face tightened into small wrinkles around his eyes and he said, "Mina, you have to trust me." I no longer listened to the translator. I knew what was going on.

Each muscle in Claudius' body tensed. Muscles in his back raised up, like neck fur does when bears get angry. I stepped back. As I watched his body harden and his back straighten, he wound up as if to pounce on a mouse. No longer weak and frail, he now moved quickly, as he ran. He stood in front of the first stone and carefully walked out to the last stone, pulling the Orb from his pocket. The Orb was flashing on and off, a harsh color of red, that even silenced the birds.

He stole the Orb from Mina! I spread my claws into the ground, making marks that represented my power. There was a point of no return when my body would unleash my speed and I would kill in seconds.

Mina stood next to my claw marks. "Pink! Claudius stole the Orb." Mina's voice was high, raspy and she was shaking inside her robes. "We must get it back!" She started to run toward the stones.

Claudius held the Orb toward the sky. His body changed, he smiled and a cloak of sapphire-blue surrounded his body. Mina instantly stopped, but I was still angry. I sat back to engage my back muscles and leaped over Mina, landing on the first stone. Claudius was not aware of any threat as I approached full bore toward his body. I landed on the last stone, grabbed the Orb away from Claudius with both paws, saying, "This is for Mina." Claudius slipped and fell into the water, hitting his head, and lay motionless. I vaguely remember what happened next as I fell in the water with the Orb in my paws. The Orb started turning colors and making a pleasant vibration that I felt throughout my body. I was transported to a time when Lily and I were sitting in a wide clearing with Mother. We just finished eating a hillside of berries. Lily and I were relaxing while Mother was walking around us, noticing everything. It was an old routine when we were young, but we were adults now. I was so pleased that we were back together.

The dream was fading as I reached the surface. Suddenly, I felt Mina pushing and pulling my body hair. She touched my ears and I finally came out of my trance. "I was with Mother! And Lily!" Mina, standing on the second stone, reached for the Orb and I reluctantly gave it back. I pulled myself up and noticed Claudius, face down in the pond, blood surrounding a gash on his head. It was strange, but my anger was gone.

"Yes, that's the Orb's magic, Pink, but we need to keep Claudius alive. Save him! I was wrong about him. We need Claudius. The Orb turned blue in his hands." I thought about what Mina said about keeping him alive and it made no difference to me. If she needs me, I will do it. I lifted his limp body from the water. His face was snow white in contrast to the blood flowing down his cheeks.

I carried him to shore and Mina blew air into his mouth until he started coughing. His face was still pale, but he was trying to breathe in, causing him to cough even more. I thought he was going to die, now gasping for air while still pushing out water from his mouth. After his body stopped jerking, he finally relaxed, but his eyes were still closed. Mina stood up and pushed his thin body up to standing. She walked him around in a circle as his color returned. She peeled off layers of her covering until she found a light gauzy material to wrap around the gash on his head.

As I walked around, I lost interest in Claudius and Mina. My only thought was being with Mother and Lily. Could I see them again by using the Orb? Where did Mina put it? I went back to the stone to see if she dropped it in the water. I continued to look and Mina shouted from shore, "Go get water, Pink." I went back to the cave and brought the tea pot back, filled with water. No sign of the Orb.

Mina took the water from me, but she did not notice that the Orb changed me. Lily and Mother were here and now they were gone, again. She was occupied with Claudius. Why? I wondered. He stole her Orb and now she was saving his life. It occurred to me that the Orb had power to give me Mother and Lily.

"Mina," I offered quietly. She said nothing, but pulled the Orb from her pocket to show me. She knew how I felt about the Orb? I dearly wanted to bring my family back, I knew she wanted her baby back and now realized why Claudius stole the Orb. Didn't he want to be with Klara? That was all he talked about.

It rained over several days, making everything damp with little light coming through the fog. Mina slowly brought Claudius back to health. He was constantly telling her he was sorry as she changed his bandage and fed him liquids. He did not look at me and I spent a lot of time in the woods, reliving my experience, over and over again. It was like I could not hear, see, smell anything else. I was stuck. I needed to know more about the Orb. Mina could now read my thoughts without the translator. She said, 'There are answers, Pink. We just have to be patient. It will all work out." I returned to the cave to the two of them whispering. Claudius was giving her information and she did not seem happy. They stopped talking and looked at me, and the side of their lips were turned down. That word trust came up to me again. I was outside, and they were talking in my cave, without me. My vision became cloudy and I felt a weird reaction to this new danger. My head was bursting with more words. Words. Trust was still the word that held me in this loop. That word was something my body was protesting.

"What's wrong?" I asked. Her head was down as if there was a heavy weight was sitting on her shoulders. Was Claudius making her feel pain? After everything she did for him?

Claudius tried to stand, but quickly fell back, sitting on the floor. "I have to talk with you, Pink."

I relaxed. I could flatten him and tear him into pieces, but I wanted more words. Was Mina in danger? "Why are you here, Claudius? You should answer this question. Why are you interested in the Orb and the stones in the pond?"

"Yes, that is a good question," said Mina.

"Please believe me. I can be trusted." Trust was now an interesting word for me. I turned that word into an example. His actions did not match his words. Trust was important now, more important than ever.

It surprised me that Mina was nodding for me to trust him as she set out to make tea. This time, the tea ceremony passed quickly. I sensed stress in their bodies and this tea was not helping.

Mina collected the cups and lay the Orb on her basket, close to the fire. She started humming a song she said was named

Blackbird. She stopped. "Claudius has information for us to think about, Pink. Each of us recognizes, firsthand, the power of the Orb. In each case, I think it connected our lives to others we loved."

Claudius nodded, but he still seemed fragile, like a delicate bird. How thin he was. "When I held the Orb, I was living inside of a dream, Pink. I was back in Austria, at an altar with Klara, my beloved. Her head was covered with her favorite wildflowers and her dress made from Belgium lace. She smiled at me with love. I cannot believe she waited to marry me. That's what I saw while I held the Orb. I woke up to find you attacking me and pushing me into the water." After he spoke, his eyes were staring straight ahead, his body softened and he smiled. He bent over, shaking, with tears flowing from his eyes.

I had a mixed reaction to his words. I wanted to split him in two and I wanted to know more about the dreams. I experienced something similar. How can I trust that he is speaking the truth? He took the Orb from Mina? What is she thinking?

Mina shifted the mood and talked about her experience, quietly and slowly as if each word was important. Yes, when she used the Orb, her baby was in her womb and she felt it move. I saw that happen, so I could trust her words. "Each time I talk about it, I think I am in the experience. Nozomu-sensei told me it was important to practice, so when the time came, I would be prepared." She then said to me, "Pink, can you tell us what you experienced?"

I felt my story. It came directly from my heart. I told it, with a lot of detail of the time of day, the smell of the wildflowers and how I felt being with my family again. As I finished, a feeling of heaviness came over me. What was I experiencing? It seemed real, as if they were sitting here today. What was this?

"Thank you, Pink," said Mina. "We know a lot more about how we each experience the Orb. We know that Dr. Nozomu said that only one of us can use it to time travel. It's complicated. Claudius, tell us what you know."

"Mina, you just saved my life and I'd like to think you saved millions of people." Claudius adjusted his position. "The Orb is special and sent us back, individually, to the most important times of our lives. These moments frame the happiness we lost and want to bring back."

He turned to me. "I know you are angry, Pink, but be patient. It is vital that you know everything. We need to work this out." At the same time, Mina, without moving a hair, looked directly in my eyes, while her face stayed motionless. I thought about everything: The disrupted hibernation, the changes Mina experienced with the Orb, Claudius stealing the Orb and my dream, sitting with Mother and Lily.

I stood up and turned to face Claudius. "Why did you steal the Orb from Mina?"

Claudius' face turned red, brightened as he finally controlled the shaking in his body. Did he know the importance of my question? "Pink, the Orb has unique powers. It will draw you toward it and if you pick it up, you will be transformed to an extraordinary feeling from your past. Just as you described. I took it because I was weak. It takes a lot of strength to resist its power. I wanted to practice on the same stone Mina did and find a way I can use the Orb to go back in time. You will find yourself drawn to the Orb again and again. Without discipline and practice, you can exhaust it before we use its one travel through time. I apologize to you and to Mina. This is very important."

I thought about the moment I picked up the Orb. I did feel that attraction. I even thought about taking the Orb from Mina to see Mother and Lily again. The power was strong. His words helped me understand why he stole from Mina. But I needed more information. What were we doing together and why was it important for the Orb to be attached or detached from us? My mind was racing.

Claudius leaned forward to pick up the Orb. The Orb's color was the pale blue of the morning sky. "Don't worry. I'm not taking this and I'm sure Pink would crush me if I did. I need to prepare for time travel and this is why.

"After my mother's death, I stayed in Spital at my family home. I reluctantly put Klara out of my mind. In the late 1930s, Adolph Hitler rose as a political figure and I realized this man was Klara's son, the baby I saw in the cradle. With no interest in politics, I ignored him as I focused on my work, not wanting to think about Klara or her son.

"As I changed my life's purpose, I became a park ranger in Austria. It fulfilled my desire to walk and be in nature as much as possible. I became quite an important figure in the Austrian walking community and led many groups to beautiful locations to take pictures and stay in Hüttes, little compact houses in the woods. In 1916, Woodrow Wilson established the first national park system in the United States, and ten years later, I was invited to visit him. Throughout my work, I traveled many times to consult with the Department of Interior to advise on managing these parks. I was a big deal. I was in the United States when the US joined the war. After much trouble establishing that I was not a spy, I applied for citizenship and have lived here since then. I'm just turning 90 this year. I do not have much time left."

'Time left,' I thought. What does that mean? 90 years meant 90 times in hibernation. I had five hibernations. Did humans live that long? They were so different in so many ways. With guns that killed in that special way, they were an animal species that could live a long time.

"I just recently met Dr. N." He paused. "He told me I could change history. If I followed his directions, I would find a Japanese woman with a globe, an Orb, is what he called it. If I went to these coordinates, I would find her preparing to use the Orb to go back in time. He told me to tell her that I was the butterfly and not her. That I would be able to cure my deepest sorrow, affect millions of lives and save one woman's life. She would be reunited with her baby.

With very little preparation, I traveled to the coordinates Dr. N. gave me and then it started to snow. I almost died. The two of you found me, and I almost died then, lying face down in the snow." He raised the Orb toward the sky and the Orb sprouted sparkling lights in blue, purple and violet. Mina's face opened up and her hands gently embraced the air. Finally, Claudius' words matched his actions, and I repeated the word, 'trust', to myself.

"Let me finish my story that is behind why we are here. When Mina left Dr. N. to go back to North Carolina with Kiko and her family, he gave her the Orb." Claudius looked straight at her. "He told me you returned to the retreat center to practice using the Orb. In order to use it for time travel, one needs to develop skills to resist its pull. Specific moves, like a dance, need to be developed. The final time travel movements had to be done during the Summer Solstice. You were planning on going back in time before August 1945 to save you and Saki. Isn't that right, Mina?"

"Yes, he trained me," said Mina. "He also sent me here too early and I was not prepared for winter. His calculation sent me to the Winter Solstice, not the Summer. I was six months too early. How did you meet him?"

"I ran into Dr. N at the Library of Congress. Klara never left my mind. She died in 1907 and thankfully, she never knew that her favorite son became the monster of the twentieth century. Living these years after World War II were unbearable for me. Slowly, after the war, more information began to come out about what Adolph Hitler did during the war. When all of the information about Adolf Hitler, Klara's son, was revealed, my life lost all meaning. I would die knowing my direct connection to the young Adolph, seeing him as a child and how my weakness in pursuing Klara resulted in his existence. I experienced depression and at my age, my life was in physical and mental decline. I could not comprehend that one man could convince an army to conduct systematic annihilation of the Jewish population. I decided I needed more information on how this happened, so I left my home in Montana and went to Washington D.C.

"As I read all of the information from the Nuremberg trials on microfiche, I met Dr. N. He was doing extensive research on the physical effects from the atom bomb on the population of Japan. He was surprised how little information there was. We shared information as we spent time using the same microfiche, letters and newspapers about World War II. Mina, I believe he was corroborating with Kiko's parents on this topic.

"These data were gruesome and the impact of radiation on the human body already showed birth defects, keloids, and cancer. So many died of side-effects from the bomb.

"We became friends and occasionally, we would go have a pint at the Old Ebbitt Grill. That was when I told him that I knew Klara, Klara Pölzl. Sitting at the bar, I even revealed my deep love for her after all of these years. I could not believe she was Adolph Hitler's mother. I even told him about my visit to the family, when Adolph was four. I told him of Klara's injuries from Alois' abusive behavior and his brother's aggressive character.

"The next morning over coffee, Dr. Nozomu asked me to visit his home in South Carolina. I was familiar with the Blue Ridge Mountain range and loved that area for hiking. While I was almost 90 years old, I still had sturdy legs and strong back from years of hiking. He promised I would not regret the trip. While he drove, we continued to talk about the research and he continued to ask me about Klara."

"You went to Dr. N's retreat center?" she asked, now staring with open eyes at Claudius.

"Mina, I was in that beautiful room you described. I also experienced the others that shared the circle and how deeply they shared their emotions. When I spoke to the circle about my last day with Klara, I felt immediate relief, finally releasing my depth of sadness and shame. I shared my weakness of not pursuing Klara before she married Alois and running away from the single most important moment in my life.

"I stayed with Dr. Nozomu and his friends a few weeks, hiked and enjoyed nature. After each walk, I returned to having long talks with Dr. Nozomu about Klara. He always listened intently and I felt better, just talking, casually and lowering my anxiety. Dr. N. kept asking me questions. He was very interested in our relationship and wondered if she returned my love. He helped me understand how natural it was for me to not be able to express my love or even know what to do at such a young age. He pointed out that I wanted what was best for her. How kind his words were toward me and I began to understand myself in a better way. We talked about what happened when she left Wisteria to become the housekeeper of Alois. He asked me when that happened and what I did about it. He exhausted each moment of my young life and was searching for some small pieces of information from every interaction I had with Klara.

"We returned to the library in Washington, completing our research on Adolf Hitler's life. He was now as obsessed as I was. We also spent a lot of time looking into the emerging statistics of World War II, the atrocities, the enormous criminal activities and finally the impact of the total death count from the war. He speculated about the loss of Jewish lives, lives of men fighting the war and the despair left behind in Europe and the United States.

"We continued our conversations in pubs and tea houses. One day, Dr. Nozomu's manner was different. He always had a casual appearance and demeanor, but this day, he was dressed formally, in a suit that had sleek lines in dark blue. That was the day he carefully explained to me the Butterfly Effect. He talked about a scientist, Edward Norton Lorenz, the mathematician and meteorologist who invented this idea in 1969. He explained to me that Lorenz's theory was backed by his calculations around chaos. His theory was that something as small as a butterfly wing in one location, could make dramatic changes someplace else in the world.

'1969? How do you know about something nineteen years from now,' I asked.

'Well, Lorenz is at MIT right now. But he won't publish this theory for a long time, nineteen years, as you pointed out. The reason I know is I'm a time traveler, Claudius.'

"I had read the *Time Machine*, by H.G. Wells in my forties, but when he said he was a time traveler, I laughed. That was until he did not smile and I realized he was serious.

"Maybe I was just too old to seriously challenge him, but it still took some convincing. What you two need to know is that I, Claudius, could change the world's future with one simple action. If I was the butterfly, my actions could change everything in a very positive direction."

Claudius stopped talking. His body relaxed, bending over and stretching his arms over his head. The mood was quiet and deep, like still pools of water. Mina was motionless. Waking up during mid-winter hibernation gave me the same feeling. I finally felt Claudius' words and how he spoke from his heart. The word trust came back to me. I wondered if this was what I was feeling about Claudius. Mina sat quietly; fully focused.

"Dr. N. often started our conversations with, 'What if Adolph Hitler was never born?' He understood the impact of my involvement with history and was easing me into thinking differently about how I saw my role." Claudius stopped talking as his eyes flooded. His shoulders shook his body and he looked across to the Orb. "He is the only person that fully understood my lifelong pain of not marrying Klara. My story convinced him that the atrocities Adolph Hitler leveled against the Jews, would not have happened, if I had followed my heart. The despair, the trauma in children's eyes, and the sickness these events poured into our civilization's memory, would disappear. That episode would not exist in books nor film. It would be extinguished from memory. All the people not killed by the German leader, Adolph Hitler, would live to create, to procreate and make our world a better place.

As Dr. N. collected information about Hitler's barbaric actions, my inner soul was completely humiliated. Dr. N. widened my pain until I realized the full extent of my folly. All the implications to millions of people who died and families that were affected, now stiffened my heart. Hearing it expressed by him, someone I admired, was painful.

"And then, when I felt utterly shamed by this information, he showed me a way to change my life, go back in time and make a difference."

CHAPTER 12

The Orb was the color of deep water, an indigo blue.

"Dr. Nozomu finally said to me, 'You are the butterfly, Claudius.'"

Mina stood up. "Nozomu-sensei told me I was the butterfly and he sent me to these coordinates, the largest rock here, with instructions of how to travel back in time to my home in Hiroshima. I spent one year practicing and planning under his direction. Does this mean I will not be reunited with my family and Saki?" Her face was wild with pain, red splotches, circling her neck.

"Mina," Claudius said as he walked toward her, "Dr. N. carefully took care of your part in this puzzle. You and Saki will be reunited, I promise. I only ask that I am allowed to finish my story." She seemed to frown, but relaxed into her folds of cloth, warming her hands in the fire.

"I had no idea what Butterfly Effect meant. After several sessions with Dr. N. explaining how it worked, I started to understand that the Orb could bring me back to a time when I would be prepared to," he paused, "effectively, marry Klara. By marrying Klara, I would change history and find my happiness. It was an unbelievable proposal. I also considered that Dr. N. was crazy, but everything he knew and the laborious way he explained things, led me to believe I could trust him. Mina, this would mean that World War II would not happen, nor an atomic bomb blasting away your home in Hiroshima. If I am successful in marrying Klara, you would have Saki and your family back. No one would be harmed. If you add up all the total loss of life from World War II, it adds up to around 70 million people, including many civilians like yourself. Actually, many, many families would be back together. Dr. N. said the lives that were saved would make a healthier future. If I followed the Orb, I would make this future happen. I never thought about making a difference this big before. You have to believe me Pink."

All of this information was dulling my mind. I needed a break and Mina headed to the corner of the cave to sit. She seemed to be dramatically affected by everything Claudius said. I wanted to ask her questions, but I decided to sit and wait and think about all of these pieces of information. I really wanted to know why I felt Mother's and Lily's presence when I held the Orb. Where were they now?

"What does the Butterfly Effect mean?" I asked Claudius. "Was being with Mother and Lily called the Butterfly Effect?

"No, Pink, that is what you feel when you hold the Orb. The Butterfly Effect, means if you go back in time, using time travel and alter one small thing, you could change the future of the world. The change can either be good or bad or neutral. For example, if I went back in time to give Klara a seed and she planted it, the balance of nature could change negatively or positively. These seeds might grow into a tree that decimates other plants and prevents them from growing. And those newly-introduced trees could cause a negative impact, maybe affecting the food supply of migrating birds, causing them to be extinct. Time travel is fragile."

Mina came back from sitting in the corner. She started talking fast, even the translator gave up as words sputtered from its plastic body. They spoke back and forth and did not wait for translations. They shouted at each other as Mina walked back and forth, looking tired. Claudius continued to sit with a straight back and did not lose his physical energy like Mina did. This all made me drowsy, and I slept.

I woke up to a stony silence, the solitude I treasured. The harsh voices were missing and nothing made a sound in the cave, except for ants and spiders. My first thought was about Claudius. Why did I accept that he would not try and harm Mina or me with his new plan? She was upset. I wasn't threatened by his elongated body, like a grasshopper, but if Mina was angry, I would help her. I then felt a warmth fill my body when I thought about Mina, my first visitor in the coldest depth of winter. Her stories, her tea, her calming manner, now reminded me of Mother. I was attached to these two humans in different ways. I was close to Mina and I would protect her to my death, but I was starting to understand that Claudius was not a threat, his body was old and he was lost without Klara. All of these thoughts came flooding in while I realized my new desire was to be close to Mina and Claudius.

The three of us went to the stone where Claudius fell. Claudius sat on the shoreline while Mina walked to the largest stone. Whatever differences they had were resolved. She held the Orb up as it pulsed, coating Mina in a sphere of sapphire-blue. She rotated it above her head and then brought it down, slowly crossing it back and forth over her body. She returned to shore and handed it to Claudius. "Think about the love you feel for Klara when you practice."

Claudius moved like an insect as he repeated Mina's movements. She watched and encouraged him to observe the Orb's color as he moved his body. That was all he needed to do. The feedback he received from the Orb glowed from deep red to sky blue. I was amazed how his body flowed in the air, like Mina's. It looked like he was scooping up the sky as he rotated up and then down toward the earth. He reversed direction and, each time, the Orb reacted by adding green, yellow, orange and finally red again. As colors were added, our bodies were soaked in a continuous rainbow that stretched across the lake. I was stunned. When Claudius stopped moving, each color disappeared one at a time until blue was left and then it dissolved in air. Mina got up and walked behind me and stretched her arms all the way around my neck. She laid her head against me and I could feel her whole body relax against my fur. My neck was wet from the water flowing from her face. This simple gesture warmed me inside.

"Eureka, I did it!" he shouted.

"That was perfect, Claudius." She pushed her body away from mine and gestured for him to come back to the shore.

With the translator on the ground and the Orb in the middle, we sat facing each other, coating our space in the Orb's glowing blue sphere of light. We were surrounded by nature's bright, bold music. Birds filled the air, insects beat their wings and plants emerged with their capes of green. But it was the wild, vibrant scent of spring that I remembered in that moment. We continued sitting, like we were close, a family, with no angry voices. This was spring, a beginning and a final parting from winter. With new growth surrounding us and a reminder of strong connections between us, the energy passed through the circle, connecting our bodies.

Mina spoke first. "Pink, we are sorry, but we had to fight with words for the truth to come out. I know Claudius feels the same way. Everything is strange, different from what I expected. There's a major shift in Nozomu-sensei's plan. We are taking steps to follow the new directions he gave Claudius. I am now convinced that the Orb will send Claudius back to marry Klara and I will be back in my body in Hiroshima, unharmed."

I was happy they no longer were angry. Something was new and I realized they were leaving. The Orb practice was about leaving. They came here so they could leave.

"You're leaving?"

"Pink, at the peak of the summer solstice, I will be transported back to Lycée, high school, with Klara and I will marry her. All of the events, including the bombing of Mina's city, would not take place without Adolph Hitler. At least, that is what Dr. Nozomu told me. He was certain that while Japan might engage in war and conflict, this one specific bomb will not happen at that time or place."

Mina and Claudius looked at each other in silent conversation. I was now anxious and had to hear more. It was impossible for me to understand. The Orb had special magic that changed lives by sending humans back in time to change their actions. Would I be able to go back and warn Mother?

"Here's what we know. Dr. Nozomu told me that anyone who holds the Orb will be reminded of the most loving part of their life. Pink, the Orb showed you Mother and Lily when you held it. The Orb would take you to that moment with Mother and Lily," said Claudius as his face became wrinkled, like he was in pain. "When Mina holds the Orb, her loving moment is when Saki is back in her belly. Dr. N. told her to practice using the Orb to summon her connection to Saki. If this is done during the Spring Equinox, the moment when darkness and light are equal, the Orb will transport anyone who stands in these coordinates back in time to their most loving moments. Performing the movements at the exact moment of Spring Equinox will reunite me with Klara. The rest is up to me. All I have to do is declare my love for her and marry her."

I looked at each of them and saw something, an excitement in their eyes, I had not seen before. My mind was filled with many thoughts and ideas, but I could not find words to explain what I was feeling. They were leaving me. I was going to lose my friends. All the adventures and stories were going away and I would remember them, just like I remembered Mother and Lily, with sadness.

"Pink, we are fulfilling a purpose that was bestowed on us by Dr. Nozomu." Mina shook her head as I tried to understand her words and she repeated that word, Purpose. The word I wondered about. "We have a purpose and we have to follow through, just as summer replaces spring. We are also sad to leave, but this idea is bigger than you and the cave. It involves the lives of many people, people we can save."

"Why does purpose make you leave?" I asked.

"It's complicated," said Claudius. "Our purpose for being here was decided a long time ago. Someone or something created the Orb for us to use. Our purpose is to save the lives of all the people who died from my mistake."

I was more confused with Claudius' explanation. "Why did people die?"

"It was a war. People killing people. The number of people that died were more than the number of leaves in the trees that we talked about. More than the number of ants in an anthill. One man was responsible for all of these deaths and this device will help us remove him in the least harmful way. Dr. Nozomu calls this the Butterfly Effect. Just in one day, 70,000 people were killed, including Mina and her baby. One man, Klara's son, Adolph, systematically annihilated 11 million lives. I now have the opportunity to not just go back and find the love of my life, but also make a big contribution in changing the future. That is my purpose."

I was stunned at how I was feeling. Mina and her baby were killed? If I had a purpose, it would be to stay with my bear family or Mina and Claudius, my new family. That was my purpose. To keep each other healthy, fed, warm and pause to hear the birds sing. I had no other purpose. I was sad and empty. My mind stopped when I thought about saving human lives. Humans that killed each other? Was that a good thing? Humans killed Mother.

"Dr. N.'s instructions did not include you, Pink. He was not aware that you were here. We wondered if you would like to go back and be with Mother and Lily. You saw them when you held the Orb. You could go back and warn Mother to stay away from the hunters. We think you would go back to the time, when you were with Lily and Mother." Mina handed me the Orb. "Take this Orb and practice the movements like Claudius did. See what happens."

I wanted to go someplace where I could sit alone and so I moved to a clearing above the rocky outcrop, looking toward the horizon. The sun was almost directly above me. As I cupped the Orb, just like the tea bowl, I immediately felt the same way as before. For a long time, I sat in the warm glow of being with Mother and Lily. The longer I held the Orb, the stronger the attraction. I could not believe we were together, and I felt warmed by the reality of their presence. Lily touched my feet just like she did when we were small. I did not want to leave.

As I sat, I realized how my surroundings changed. I missed the bird's spring song, the many bird voices fading. The grasses around me smelled dry and faded. While I was sitting with my family, everything else turned gray and black. As I placed the Orb in front of me, the strong attraction created a strength, something without words that started inside me. The woods lived around me again. Mother and Lily were gone. I sat and continued to become stronger. Just when the sun showed mid-afternoon, I was able to walk back, carrying the Orb. I found Claudius on the last stone.

He looked back and forth, across the lake. The sun was just setting, a bright ball, sinking into the horizon, between two trees. "We need to be here when the sun rises. When the sunrise is directly opposite of the sunset, where those two tall trees are," he then pointed in the opposite direction, "that is the Spring Equinox and that is when we must be ready to use the Orb. Are you going to join us, Pink?"

I placed the Orb on the large stone where Claudius was sitting. "No. I'm staying here, on my land and around my cave. I will move forward without Mother. Bears have to be themselves and live their lives, separate from their mothers. I think that is what she meant for me to do."

Claudius nodded and we sat together on the stone until dark. The next morning, the sun rose above the trees. We all studied the tall cottonwood and the bright fresh, yellow ball as it rose behind the tree, tracing its path toward its highest point. It was almost time.

They went back to the cave and collected their things, moving with precision. Mina pulled lots of fabric out of her bag and put on the many layers of her kimono. Claudius mentioned that his younger body was stronger and bigger and his clothing would be too tight. Mina folded the hanten jacket, put a yellow daisy on it and placed it toward the back of the cave. She left the tea pot and bowls as well.

She knew my decision without asking. We hugged each other many times. Tears were dropping from their faces. Mina's calm white face was wet, but Claudius' face was shiny and red. I wished I could cry too, but I experienced sadness in a different way, returning to that old feeling I had about Mother.

They had been discussing the correct procedure. Claudius' information was more recent. Dr. N. was clear that Mina would go back in time weeks before the bomb. If Claudius did not marry Klara, Mina would still be able to move far away from the epicenter and Saki would live.

Mina's face was wet as she hugged me around the neck and said, "I love you, Pink." As the sun was almost at its peak, they walked to the stones. Claudius was jumpy and stepped up onto the largest stone, holding the Orb, while Mina followed. Looking for the exact solstice moment, the Orb seemed to be guiding his movements while Mina watched. The sapphire glow continued, until it covered the entire lake, He repeated the movements, but nothing happened. He spoke to himself with Mina saying quiet words about slowing down. He repeated each movement carefully, and when he finished, he disappeared, as did Mina.

I looked for the Orb, but it was no longer on the stone. I was hoping for one last glimpse of Mother. I just sat for a long time and listened to the birds in a new way. Each sound was slow and I could now hear things more clearly.

It was just like when Lily left me, only something was different this time. These people had purpose. I was not sure what that was, and I might think about it later. These wild humans. I would miss them. I sat there until sunset and the moment when the sun rays were squeezed out by darkness. I was tired, returned to the cave and fell asleep.

My moments alone extended to hours and then days. I had no information whether Claudius or Mina found the love that they so dearly wanted. Did they make a difference? I only knew that no shots from hunters took place that fall. My preparation for winter was slightly different. I collected more firewood, protected the bowls by arranging them in the way Mina would and even dried out the lower areas of the cave from standing water. I wondered if Mina would return.

CHAPTER 13

by Dr. Nozomu, 6/19/1952

The penalty for conducting the Soul Transformation Project without permission was severe. We did not think that anyone would care or even be able to trace what we did. We tinkered, a wonderful word I learned from this era, with different approaches in removing a human soul from a body during a catastrophic event into a soulless body, e.g. in a coma. The device we used was called ST-3, Soul Transformation, rev #3. It was the farthest along and most promising. The catastrophic event we selected was from the past. The atom bomb of Hiroshima, the end of WWII, was at a precise time of day and lives were decimated immediately. This small trial would only capture a small number of souls from bodies affected close to the epicenter of the bomb. We were very, very cautious not to cause the dreaded Butterfly Effect or change history significantly for this first trial. We convinced ourselves that moving souls into bodies in a coma would not make a big difference. The year we started the experiment and when my life changed forever was 2550.

While our activities were small and inconsequential, we took many precautions against being caught. There were copious laws written about time travel protocol. Anything that changed the future was called the Butterfly Effect. If a violation occurred, well-documented penalties were in place and strictly enforced. The BEC (Butterfly Effect Council) was the legal body that monitored and prosecuted anyone that modified the future using time travel in the past. Any proposed research using time travel had to be submitted to the BEC. If a proposal is approved after three BEC committee reviews with an 'A' rating, the work can start. Any proposal that fails to receive an 'A' rating would have to repeat the full process over. It was rare, but over the years, some carefully controlled experimental time travel proposals received an A rating, but were never conducted. The submittal process being so extensive, most projects failed due to a lack of funds. Needless to say, we never submitted. Looking back on our actions, we would be considered renegades in the twentieth century, which is another reason I want to detail what happened in this report and in Pink's account.

Our project team was highly motivated when they discovered Soul Transformation. I led a research team that allowed for many directions of research. The team went wild when a young physics student discovered the use of activation energy to separate the soul from the body. With extraordinary efforts and funding, this cohesive group discovered a way to transfer the soul to a new body. They found souls transferred best when they could do it during a catastrophic event that was well defined. The only way for them to do this was go to the past and find a body that would be decimated at a precise time. Only then could they use the ST device to make this swap just seconds after the catastrophic event. Therefore, we needed to set a small trial in the past to determine if it would be successful.

This small trial would not be detectable unless the future changed. We had to measure changes before and after the trial to demonstrate that the ST device worked. Our device was sent five hundred feet from the epicenter of the Hiroshima bomb, minutes after the bomb was dropped from the Enola Gay. According to our calculations, any living human being in this area would be a candidate. Upon completion of the project, we checked against all databases and determined the ST device did not change history and we concluded that no BE occurred. One mistake we did make was not being able to trace the souls, if any, that were transferred. The Orb, invented in 2110 by Dr. M. Kawaguchi, a Japanese woman, was sent with the ST Device to record what happened, but it did not travel with the ST. We didn't have a record of what happened, just the comparison that a BE did not take place.

We were disappointed and started working on the next experiment with better measuring capability. We were wildly enthusiastic with ourselves until someone on the Butterfly Effect Council (BEC) discovered our time travel experiment.

A trial quickly transpired. My wife held up her hands in prayer, I stood tall and braced for what they were going to say. We showed our data and concluded no traces of BE occurred.

I think they were going to go easy on us until Dr. Simonsen, a finicky old codger, another favorite word from the 50s, who loved to execute his authority over rule-breakers, asked questions. He never invented anything, so never understood the risk a scientist must take these days to get anything done. Ultimately, he asked me how many souls were transferred and where did they go? I was the leader and I was taking complete responsibility for the whole team. And of course, I was not able to answer either question.

I was found guilty of the Butterfly Effect, violating Code 62666. Before sentencing, I suggested that I go back in time and undo anything related to the ST device. This involved going back to find the souls that were transferred and undo what was done. I showed them a newer device invented by the team called the Blue Orb and the benefits it had. It was equipped with time travel, a built-in receiver for locating STs and additional properties too numerous to mention. If they accepted my proposal, I would go back in time myself and reverse anything that happened, using the Blue Orb.

Instead of sentencing, I was given a chance to reverse everything we did. Dr. Simonsen's main concern was eliminating any chance of a BE. If I went back in time and reversed the whole experiment, I might be found not guilty. Any ST that occurred would be sent back to their original location, to the epicenter, just before the bomb took place. This would ensure no BE took place. The soul would stay with the body and both would be decimated from the atom bomb that was released. They agreed with my proposal, but warned me of the serious penalty if I was not successful. I had no choice but to try and I was sent back to the year, 1939.

The following is a Summary Judgement from the trial, authored by Dr. Simonsen:

"Nozomu-sensei was sent back in time to identify STs from the Hiroshima bombing and completely reverse any interference the ST created and send those souls back to their original bodies and locations. While Nozomu-sensei identified only one Soul Transformation, Mina Kawaguchi, the defendant did not fulfill the requirement we asked for. That is your first violation of Code 62666.

In addition to that serious violation, Dr. N. also chose to send Claudius Siefert Mannheim back in time with instructions to follow his heart and marry Klara Pölzl. This changed history completely, in a very significant way. This was the second serious violation of BEC standards. This is your second violation of Code 62666.

Before I conclude with your sentencing, several members want to comment that your second violation was intriguing. Some members of the committee said it was almost brilliant in eliminating Adolph Hitler from the history books, without killing him. We've received proposals to go back in time and kill Adolph Hitler, increasing our population in a much-needed way, but we have never come across anyone who would change history in such a non-violent, effective manner.

Had you made a proposal to the BEC for review, we are certain if all other requirements were met, you might have received an A rating.

Regardless of the positive impact of Nozomu-sensei's actions, we voted 3:2, that Nozomu-sensei violated Code 62666 and our specific directions for him to eliminate any chance of a BE effect. We cannot be lenient in this matter.

Verdict: Guilty of violating Code 62666

Sentence: Nozomu-sensei will return to the past and never return. Dr. Nozomu has ten days to prepare to serve sentence.

My sentencing was now complete, and I was banished to live in the past, leaving my family, permanently. Knowing the vote was close gave us hope that the sentence could be appealed and my Butterfly Effect would be accepted. I supplied the committee with all the data Claudius and I collected. I remember how low his energy was when he discovered the full extent of the atrocities committed by Klara's son, Adolph. Those details, the number of deaths including civilians and some of the first hand conversations we had with survivors of what was called the Holocaust, were summarized.

Before I left, my wife and I talked about how to communicate about the children or my parents, but unfortunately, there was no way to communicate with each other and we would have to live with this uncertainty until the committee reconvened again. Her astrophysics background helped me understand that if the BE took place, I would be removed from the past and appear one day in the future. She warned me it would be instantaneous and whatever I was doing or wearing would go with me. We had a laugh over that.

As of June 19, 1952, I'm stranded, exiled to the past, by almost 300 years. Each morning, as I recall the age of each of my children, I'm reminded that I gave up my life for the good of mankind. Looking at it less altruistically, I live by my own principles and this is what I want my life to look like. I send love energy to each child and my wife across time, hoping they would receive it.

While I was tinkering with a device to track Claudius, I discovered the translator was left behind. I was surprised at this, as I told Claudius to destroy it. Leaving it for someone to discover would have dire consequences with additional sentencing added to my current crimes. I decided to retrieve it.

I set out for the coordinates I gave Mina and Claudius in January. Upon arrival, I had no idea that winter here was so fierce. Winter did not exist in the future and I had not paid much attention to weather conditions for these coordinates. My laboratory was located here in the year 2550, a concrete building with twelve stories. Unbeknownst to me, in the year 1952, these coordinates were positioned in a deep woods. My second shock was it was winter with snow and cold, which I had to walk through, unprepared. I wondered how Mina survived it and even Claudius.

When I arrived at these coordinates, it had just snowed, big white flakes landing softly, it was fluffy and white. Not until the temperature went below zero Celsius did I realize the danger I was in. It was colder than I had ever experienced.

Finding the translator was easy, but digging in the snow for it was not. It was encapsulated in ice and my hands were a bright red, almost too numb to turn it on. My body temp was lowering dangerously, but I needed to know what happened. With the volume turned up, I was able to listen to conversations that were translated from the very first words. Hearing Mina say, 'My name is Mina. What is your name?', was mystifying. It was a wild ride after that.

To whom was she speaking? I continued to listen and was riveted. Finally, I concluded that she was speaking to a bear, a bear called Pink, who was either pink or albino. This information was fascinating, but also meant I would find this cave someplace close.

This, hopefully, would save me from a horrible death. I stopped the recording and walked around until I found the cave, the entrance also encrusted in snow. Using the very end of my strength, I was just barely able to break a small sheath of ice. Suddenly, the icy shroud collapsed. I stood peering into the dark space and had to make a decision. I would die if I stayed out and the firepit was a welcome sight with the pile of dry wood next to it. I took a step into the cave.

I was no longer shaking with cold, but with fear. I made myself small, but this albino bear was in front of me, digging into the dirt with claws the size of my arm. My nose was in front of the first log of the firepit and I had to choose. Start a fire or freeze to death. This bear could tear me apart, but I was going to die of cold, anyway.

It took a long time, but he finally settled back in the corner after looking at me. If I was to guess, he was in some stage of hibernation that produced dream states and since my small body showed no signs of harm, he must have just settled back. Hibernation is critically important to the life cycle of bears. I waited until his body functions slowed.

As the temperature of my toes increased, my feet were burning with pain. To distract myself, I retrieved the translator to listen to the rest of the story. After listening to everything, I realized that Pink would awaken for the Winter Solstice, a practice that his mother, Mother, created for her family. He awoke on the day when night and daylight hours are equal, the Winter Solstice. How strange, I thought, but I got ready and repeated every detail of the ritual with him. Finally, I made the tea and said, "Pink, my name is Dr. Nozomu."

Pink showed no interested in using the translator I believe he recognized my name but he went to the back corner of the cave and laid down to sleep.

Spring was when Pink woke up. I was ready to have my first conversations with a bear. We started slowly, but he was very interested in what happened to Mina and Claudius. Pink and I spent time together until the Spring Equinox which marked one year after Claudius and Mina's Time Travel. We talked into the translator a lot and I began to understand him beyond the words coming from the translator.

Listening to what happened in this cave and how they opened up to Pink, using this translator, was astounding or flabbergasting, as they would say in the 50s. I've recorded all of the conversations, sprinkling it with Pink's point of view, which helped me come to grips with what I have done. Trust was as important to him as to me. I have to trust that I did what was right for civilization. Communicating with Pink was the most important time of my life. I left him, saying I would return. My wife and I laughed, knowing that at any moment I might be transferred forward in time.. If that happened, I would miss him terribly.

CHAPTER 14

My heart was slow, to the beat of snow, falling in my winter dreams. Sleeping was uneven and sometimes disturbing. Images of Mina's blue robes and Claudius' thin profile seemed to take away from my dreams of Mother and Lily. So much happened to me that my mind was full. I needed to restock and rest in the deep, winter cold. Occasionally, I would wake and listen and even use words in my dreams. Words that I used with my new family. If I stayed awake longer, I would wonder. What happened? Did the Orb change Claudius and Mina? Did they find their loved ones? What changed with the evil man, Adolph, they spoke about? This was the end Claudius wanted. I trusted his desire to go back to Klara and to take Mina with him, but they were gone now.

When I stayed awake, more questions arose. I always thought about Mother and Lily and my decision not to find them in time. Why didn't I go? This question disturbed me most, but I still fell back into a heavy hibernation. As my heart would slow, my dreams softened to finding Mina sitting at the entrance of the cave, with her black hair against her blue robe, dripping wet.

My heart started beating faster, at a pace that I remembered from Mina's winter visit. Then there was a sound, as if she was outside the walls of the cave. I remembered the slow, soft crunch of snow. I heard more steps. If this was Mina, joy would arrive with her. I would be happy to warm her with a fire and make tea. I found a new plant that gave off a woody, earthy smell. It would please Mina.

I first looked for the deep blue of her cloak and finally, as my eyes adjusted, there was a human standing outside the cave, as tall as Claudius, but different. He shook in the cold as humans did from the hard icy snow blasts. This human was standing, pushing his hands against the ice, opening a small space, when the whole ice barrier broke apart, leaving this dark figure. He stepped into the cave and I moved fast, claws out, ready to strike.

With my new sense around humans, I knew he could not harm me. I relaxed to sitting and looking at him. His skin was red from cold and his dark hair reminded me of Mina's. He looked malnourished like Claudius, so I knew he would not survive outside.

He went right to making a fire. He didn't use the proper placement of logs that Mina repeated so many times, but it was fire. I went back to my corner, saddened by the fact that Mina did not return. He was not important enough for me to worry about but he seemed familiar. I would think about him later and fell back to sleep.

I was awake, my heartbeat increasing, slowly. I lifted my head to look around. There he was, making tea on this day, Mother's

Winter Solstice ritual. He arranged things in their proper place and started to recite her poem into the translator.

Long nights of winter

Getting shorter

Find your wild dreams

No fear

Peace and courage

Stay wild.

Yes, the translator! I had forgotten about it. The idea that this was part of dreaming was strong. I was not fully awake, but seeing this man, his body so similar to Mina, preparing the tea, made sense. He took a bag from the corner and layered it so he could sit off the dirt. The fire blazed strong and he was sitting, repeating the words of the Winter Solstice into the translator again.

I remembered Mother's soft gaze on me when I first learned her poem. He finally spoke to me, using the translator.

"Pink, my name is Dr. Nozomu."

He knew my name? My ritual? The location of my cave? I'm not dreaming?

Just as if Mina was there, I did not react, I was tired. My dreams gave me Mina, Mother and Lily and I wanted to go back.

At times, I opened my eyes, always seeing this man. Sometimes sleeping, but most of the time, holding the translator to his ear.

Finally, refreshed, I opened my eyes to a day of spring. He was still there and gave me a plate of dried berries and nuts. I sat and wondered why I was still dreaming, but there was the translator, between us. I was not dreaming, this man was real! Why didn't I fear him? He could cause danger, maybe he captured Mina.

"I'll make tea and we can talk," he said. He made tea his way, not as smooth. I watched him and he was stiff like Claudius and suddenly, I realized that he was wearing the jacket Mina left behind. And I remembered that jacket was given to her by Dr. N. This was his jacket.

"Where is Mina?" The question rushed out of the translator, as my fur was rising along my spine.

"Pink, I can only hope she is okay. I hope Mina is with Saki now and her family. If Claudius went back in time to marry Klara, we will know soon. His changes will be dramatic. If they are successful, I will disappear."

I thought about his words and sat for a long time. He sat and watched me. I was confused. "What happened?"

"I will tell you about everything. You asked about Mina. I've been listening to every conversation you had with Mina and Claudius. The translator recorded everything and that helped me understand what happened here."

"Are they okay?"

"Yes, I'm hoping everything worked out. We are waiting for a decision that will put everything in place. I'm sorry to disturb you from your hibernation, but I had to locate the translator. I now know what happened. They both used the Orb that day, but you did not. You could have gone back to save Mother. The hold the Orb had for you was strong, but you decided not to go back in time."

I paused and realized how much this man, Dr. Nozomu, knew about me. It was uncomfortable, but I knew his name so well. They all spoke about Dr. N., and here he was.

We spent some time with the translator. I forgot how confusing words were for me, after months of not using them. We sipped tea and said many words back and forth.

"Let me explain," he said. "As I sent Claudius to follow Mina to this location, I was not aware of your presence."

I left the cave for a while to study what just happened. I was getting used to being alone and did not like having another human here. Humans were a lot of work and I wanted to live alone, but he stayed.

We spent months together until the Spring Equinox, when daylight and nighttime were equal. He parted shortly after that. He said, hopefully, he would not return.

Dr. N. never returned. I spent a lot of time wondering where he was and where Mina and Claudius went. These were special humans. I met other bears and heard Lily had cubs and followed a group bears moving north. I'm thinking I may follow them too.

ACKNOWLEDGEMENTS

"This is not the time to stay at home,
but to go out and give yourself to the rose garden."
–Jalal-ud-Din Rumi

Rumi was half right, give yourself to the rose garden. The second half of this pandemic produced a second book on the heels of, "Lazarus Rising," while staying at home. Support in this endeavor required extraordinary care from a few that wanted this story come to life, with the provision that I only if I give myself to the rose garden. In short, this support allowed me to explore relationship between sentient beings and humans. For that, I am forever grateful.

The beginning of the book was not a book at all. It was at a retreat where we selected clay to roll between our hands while meditating. I selected pink and thought about Teutonic shifts as I palmed the clay into a flat surface and finally looked down at it and there was a pink bear before me.

I want to thank both organizations and individuals for inspiration, encouragement, suggestions and wild ideas. Deb Byers, Anna Maria Paleocrassas, Hannah Cunningham, Kathy Giorgio, Jody Semchuk, David King, The Cocos, Geneen Hogan, Doug Van Houten, Animas Valley Institute, The Women's leadership Community, Mindful Self Compassion (MSC) and Making Friends with Yourself (MFY).

ABOUT THE AUTHOR

Author photo by Riedel Photo

Sharon K. Grosh, an author writing her second novel inspired by a love of challenging reality in an allegorical magical realism takes into a world of Pink bears, and two characters following their hearts. This unusual approach to fiction is called *Capturing The Butterfly*, the second book published by Black Rose Writing.

Sharon lives in Afton, Minnesota and divides her time between writing, mixed media, growing natural dyes, teaching meditation and creating Indigo-Shibori fabric wall hangings.

NOTE FROM THE AUTHOR

Word-of-mouth is crucial for any author to succeed. If you enjoyed *Capturing the Butterfly*, please leave a review online—anywhere you are able. Even if it's just a sentence or two. It would make all the difference and would be very much appreciated.

Thanks!
Sharon K. Grosh

ALSO BY SHARON K. GROSH

As nuclear bombing pulverizes everything above ground, find out how five individuals experience the catastrophe in the tunnels below the surface. This book walks, then runs, moment to moment, starting with a typical day in five ordinary lives, through a global catastrophic event.

Luming finds his comfortable life in conflict with lessons imprinted on him by his Chinese mother. Jane, a dealmaker, has a quirky hobby of preparing for catastrophes. Dan, is an off-beat corporate executive facing retirement. Lois, postgraduate in Mandarin and statistics, creates algorithms around spiderweb designs. Michael is a narcissistic corporate attorney whose bread and butter is sabotaging deals.

Realistic and gripping, the story describes the impact of a devastating nuclear event on the lives of these five individuals – the steps they must take and the moral dilemmas that are created just by being alive. As civilization emerges, individuals break free of fragile cultural structures to provide hope toward a nascent future. This book presents a unique perspective into corporate America, scientific innovation, and underground marijuana growers and seed-savers.

We hope you enjoyed reading this title from:

Subscribe to our mailing list – *The Rosevine* – and receive **FREE** books, daily deals, and stay current with news about upcoming releases and our hottest authors.
Scan the QR code below to sign up.

Already a subscriber? Please accept a sincere thank you for being a fan of Black Rose Writing authors.

View other Black Rose Writing titles at
www.blackrosewriting.com/books and use promo code
PRINT to receive a **20% discount** when purchasing.